DARE TO RESIST

Dare Nation Novel #1

NEW YORK TIMES BESTSELLING AUTHOR

Carly Phillips

DARE TO RESIST

He's about find a baby on his doorstep ... and his assistant in his bed.

Austin Prescott is a lot of things. Ex football player. Sports agent. And as of this morning? Father. Finding a baby on his doorstep should have been a joke but the pink sticky note and baby carrier she came in is deadly serious.

What's an out of his depth bachelor to do? Call his tempting and beyond gorgeous executive assistant and beg her to move in.

Quinnlyn Stone agrees to help Austin until he can straighten out his messy life. It's just another item on her very long To-Do list. It's absolutely not because she's attracted to her very single and extremely handsome boss.

Close quarters. A baby. Undeniable chemistry. What could possibly go wrong?

A complete standalone novel!

Prologue

Austin Prescott sat in the offices of Dare Nation, the newly minted sports agency he'd opened with Paul Dare, a man he'd grown up considering like a father to him. Instead he and his siblings had recently discovered that *Uncle Paul* was their biological dad courtesy of sperm donation. Life was crazy. But then in the Dare world, it probably fell under the definition of normal. Family came in all shapes and sizes.

And in Austin's family, he was to be the kidney donor for Paul in two weeks, which meant his need to find an assistant was urgent. He tapped his foot impatiently, in no mood to deal with yet another interview. He'd spoken to enough women in the last week to make his head spin, and he still hadn't found the right fit.

He needed someone who could keep up with negotiations and someone who could sit at the fanciest restaurants with players and their wives who thought their shit didn't stink, all while being smarter than anyone else in the room. Except for him, of course. And someone who could handle the office while he was out on medical leave.

So far he'd interviewed Ivy League graduates with attitude and average students with MBAs who just wanted an in to meet and fuck a sports star. And Austin had plenty of experience with the latter. Hell, since his Division One NCAA days followed by his NFL career, he could bed any female he wanted, but he had to admit, easy lays were getting old. He wasn't ready to settle down, but his days of picking up women every weekend were becoming fewer and farther between. Not that he was a monk, far from it. A man had needs.

He lifted his phone to let Bri, his publicist sister who'd been helping him out until he could find an assistant, know that he wanted to cancel whoever was left for the day and start over tomorrow when a knock sounded on his office door.

"Come in!" he called out, wondering why his sibling felt the need to knock.

"Mr. Prescott?" an unfamiliar feminine voice that went straight to his cock asked as she stepped inside and blew his mind. "The woman at the desk outside said I should just knock."

A gorgeous vision in a slim black skirt and a white blouse that should have looked like a uniform but instead had him wanting to bend her over his desk stepped into the room.

His gaze slid down to black pumps with enough of a heel to elongate those sexy tanned legs. Legs he wouldn't mind having wrapped around his waist as he fucked her senseless. Because from the tips of her toes to the top of her shoulder-length raven-colored hair, she epitomized class and perfection personified. The red lipstick merely added to her appeal.

"Mr. Prescott?" she asked, causing him to realize he'd been staring.

"Yes. I'm sorry. I wasn't expecting another applicant this afternoon. Ms...."

"Quinnlyn Stone but everyone calls me Quinn."

He rose to his feet, hoping she didn't notice the tent in his pants. "Nice to meet you, Quinn." He extended his hand as she stepped forward. No sooner had she slid her cool palm against his than a jolt of unexpected electricity sparked between them.

Shit. This was bad. Very, very bad. He could not desire a woman who might work for him.

"Have a seat," he said in a gruff voice, gesturing to the dual chairs across from his desk.

"Thank you." She walked over and lowered herself into one, sliding her legs to one side.

Like he thought, classy, unlike the many women who'd deliberately crossed and uncrossed their legs in an effort to draw his attention to their ... assets.

She reached into her bag and pulled out a sheet of

paper. "My resume, in case you didn't have a copy in front of you," she said.

"I appreciate you being prepared." And since he hadn't been paying attention to who his next candidate was and had hoped to cancel, he really did need the information. He accepted the resume and read through the page. "University of Miami undergrad and business school," he said, impressed with her education. "So where are you from?" He met her emerald gaze, held captive by the depths of those green eyes.

"Florida born and raised. I couldn't go far from home. My family needed me," she said somewhat cryptically.

"I see." It wasn't his business to ask why, though he was intrigued.

"I went on partial scholarship. As you can see, I graduated cum laude."

He'd noticed her honors degree. "And before this, you had a position with the Panthers," he said of the minor league team where she'd been an assistant to an assistant.

She rolled her shoulders. "It's called the ladder to success for a reason. I had to start somewhere. I have my letters of recommendation here, too." She leaned down to reach inside her purse again.

"No need. I'll look them over eventually. So you like sports?"

She nodded. "I come from a big family on both sides. A lot of siblings, cousins, uncles, everyone's a sports fan. I learned early."

He rolled a pen between his palms. "I hear you. My family was and is big on sports as well."

"You think? Two NFL players, an MLB star, a sports publicist sister … it's impressive."

The first candidate who'd truly done her research. He was impressed right back. "So why do you want this job, Quinn? Better yet, what qualifies you over the other equally competent applicants I've seen today?" He hoped she'd stutter over her words or in some way give him a reason not to hire her so he could ask her out instead.

A wry smile pulled at those sexy lips. "Well, let's see. I'm organized, efficient, and I can corral a band of preschoolers, which means I'm certain I can handle arrogant athletes."

He raised an eyebrow. "Stereotype much?"

A pretty flush rose to her cheeks, but she didn't duck her head or look away. "If the shoe fits…"

He liked this sassy woman. "So you're saying because I played football…"

"And were a Heisman Trophy winner, Rookie of the Year, and three-time Super Bowl winner that you're arrogant? Yes. Or else you wouldn't be the man sitting behind that desk today." She folded her hands in her lap and waited for his reply.

Not only had she done her homework, she looked him in the eye and was unafraid to stand up to him. "You're hired."

She blinked in surprise. "I'm sorry, what did you just say?"

He rose to his full height. "I said, you're hired. When can you start? Because I'm having major surgery in two weeks and I need someone to hold down the fort while I'm gone. Keep the clients calm and all that."

Those red lips he had plenty of uses for, in his imagination anyway, opened and closed twice before she composed herself and stood. "I can start whenever you need me. And thank you, Mr. Prescott."

"We're going to be working closely together, so call me Austin."

"Thank you, Austin."

He inclined his head. "We'll see if you're still thanking me once you've dealt with many of the juveniles I call clients. Your assessment of arrogant wasn't far off the mark."

She laughed, the sound one that would be a bright light in this office. Jesus, he was in trouble.

He strode around the desk and came up beside her. "You can talk to Bri outside. She'll take you down to our office manager, who will have you fill out paperwork and get you settled. Can you start the day after tomorrow? That'll give us time to get you up to speed before I'm out for at least five weeks. Maybe six." It sucked but his body needed to adapt to having one kidney. The doctors had warned him about exhaustion most of all.

He glanced at her and she was still in shock. Since the salary and benefits had been laid out in the job description, he didn't need to go over those details.

Finally she nodded, her eyes wide, her expression brimming with excitement. "I'm looking forward to it. Thanks again." She spun and headed out the door, leaving him behind in a floral haze of lust and need for a woman he wouldn't be able to touch.

As long as she worked for him, his motto would be hands off. Or hands on his cock, since he had a feeling he'd be jerking off to thoughts of Quinnlyn Stone at least once or twice before he got his inappropriate need for her out of his system.

Austin glanced at his Rolex, one of the first gifts he'd bought for himself once he signed his original NFL contract, and counted down the minutes. It didn't take long for Bri to let herself in without knocking.

"I thought you were taking Quinn to meet with Lindsay," he said of their office manager.

"Already handled." His sister was the fixer of the

family, mediating arguments amongst the four Prescott male siblings and occasionally their father, Jesse, when he'd been alive, like a pro. Her becoming a sports publicist was a natural choice after dealing with her family for years.

Bri plopped into the chair Quinn had been seated in earlier. "So that was a fast hire. What did you see in her that was different? Beyond the fact that she's gorgeous and exactly your type?" Bri waggled her eyebrows. "Since I know you wouldn't misbehave at work or hire her because you're attracted to her."

"Wiseass," he muttered. "Quinn has the balls to handle the job," he said bluntly.

"And handle you?"

He grinned. "She called me an arrogant athlete and proceeded to back up her claim. I'd say she's perfect for the job."

"Great! Now are you ready for surgery?" Bri leaned forward, resting her elbows on the desk. "We all got tested to be Uncle Paul's donor but you drew the lucky straw." She shook her head. "Do we still call him Uncle Paul? It's all so weird."

She bit down on her lower lip, a habit he remembered from childhood.

"Yeah. We had a father." Jesse Prescott, who'd died when Austin was twenty-one, had been a decent parent to Austin, the natural-born athlete, to Damon, also a football talent, and to Bri, the only girl.

But to Jaxon, who'd preferred baseball to a contact sport, and to Bri's twin, Braden, the brain of the bunch and now a doctor, Jesse Prescott had been a hard-ass and often mean. Which meant they were all processing the sperm donor biological father news in different ways. But there'd never been a question that if any of them were a perfect match, they'd donate a kidney to the man who had always been there for them in ways their father hadn't.

"I can handle a little surgery," he assured her.

"It's not little, Austin." Bri looked up at him with a worried expression.

"It'll be fine. Go check on Quinn. Make sure she has all her questions answered before she leaves for the day."

"Worried about her already?" Bri asked.

He rolled his eyes. "Go!"

Bri popped up from her seat and headed out. "I'll be around for you if you get nervous or anything, you know?"

He glanced at the sister he loved. "Yeah, Bri. I know."

* * *

Quinn sat alone in a conference room as she filled out myriad forms, shocked she could focus on anything after being alone with Austin Prescott and all that testosterone. She'd thought she'd been ready to meet him. After all, she'd done her research, Googling him before she arrived for her interview. She hadn't lied about her family's interest in sports, but the bulk of her current knowledge came from digging around online about Dare Nation's clients and Austin Prescott himself.

But the online photos hadn't prepared her for the man in person. He had chiseled features and tanned skin. Dark lashes framed unique indigo eyes. He had full lips she could imagine kissing and a strong, built body beneath his suit, making him the whole package.

"Whew." She waved a hand in front of her still-flushed face. Her entire body heated in an inappropriate response to her boss.

She swallowed hard and filled in her social security number on the iPad with the forms the office manager had supplied, reminding herself this was her dream job. One she wouldn't mess up because her boss was hot. She'd grown up being a pseudo-mom to her bucketload of siblings and cousins. If not for her scholarship, she'd have attended college and business school wholly on student loans because her parents couldn't afford to send all of her siblings to school on their salaries.

She had no intention of being a nanny, despite

how well qualified she might be. She loved office work and she intended to make the most of this prime opportunity. She'd pay off her student loans and have an independent life she could be proud of.

Besides, even if she'd met Austin under normal circumstances and had the same intense attraction, he wasn't the right kind of guy for her. Austin Prescott was a player and not just on the field. In his NFL days, he'd been the consummate ladies' man, never having a girlfriend, always seen with a different gorgeous woman on his arm. Actresses, models, perfect-looking females who fit his alpha-male image. Now that he was an agent to the stars, he was more discreet but no less discriminating in taste.

Quinn wasn't vain. She'd been told she was pretty, but she didn't work at it the way Austin's typical woman did. And she had no reason to be thinking about herself and Austin linked in any way at all except professional, she thought, and continued to fill out the employment forms.

* * *

Austin wasn't shocked when Quinn arrived at the office at eight a.m. on her first day. He'd said nine. She obviously wanted to make sure she had time to settle in before he put her to work. So far so good. No complaints on his end except for how much he desired her, but he knew better than to act on it and make her uncomfortable.

She obviously favored those slim skirts that showed off her ass and legs, and her silk tops wrapped perfectly around her curves. So, yeah, his head was on things other than work, but he had to get his shit together.

He'd been talking to his sister about his upcoming surgery and time off, and returning to his office, he passed Quinn's desk and paused. "Everything okay?" he asked her.

She nodded. "I'm doing as you suggested, reading through client files and getting to know about them."

"I have lunch with my brother Damon at twelve thirty, more business than personal. Join us. You can meet your first arrogant athlete," he said with a grin. "Other than me."

She shook her head and blushed. "You're not going to let me live that down, are you?"

"Probably not." He chuckled and headed into his office to go over a current contract that had already been vetted by the firm's lawyer.

An hour later, they were standing at a table with his youngest brother. "Quinn, this is Damon, my youngest brother. Damon, my new executive assistant, Quinn Stone." Austin made the introductions.

When Damon first looked at Quinn, his eyes

opened wide with approval before he quickly schooled his features. Their mother would kick both their asses if they treated any woman with less than complete respect.

"It's nice to meet you, Quinn. How are you managing working for this guy?" Damon jerked his thumb toward Austin.

"I just started but I'm enjoying myself so far."

Austin held out a chair and she settled into it.

"So Austin tells me you play football," she said. "And from what I've read, you're a quarterback for the Miami Thunder?"

"Best there is. But I'm in the last year of a three-year contract and I need it to go well. And I also need my agent to kick some managerial ass when the time comes and get me the contract I deserve." Damon followed his words with an arrogant smirk.

At the thought, Austin met Quinn's gaze and grinned. "Does he fit the mold?"

"To a T," she said, laughing.

He liked the sound.

"Why do I feel like I'm the only one not in on the joke?" Damon asked, looking from Quinn back to Austin.

"Quinn thinks she's got us athletes pegged, and you just proved her right."

"Can I get you something to drink?" a waitress

asked, leaning in very close to Austin. So close her breast brushed against his sport jacket.

It was typical when they were out. Women picked one or the other brother to flirt with. Austin had seen her assessing them from behind a support beam, making her choice. Given the nine-year age difference between them, Austin at thirty-four, Damon at twenty-five, the woman had to have a type in order to choose. That and she looked a little older than the typical groupies who picked Damon.

Quinn's eyebrows lifted high. She wasn't used to how blatant the come-ons could be. If she was going to do her job, she'd get accustomed to seeing it.

"Excuse me but I'd like to order, too?" Quinn deliberately called the woman's attention away from Austin, and he had to wonder if she was doing him a favor or if there was a touch of jealousy involved.

The waitress straightened and barely glanced at Quinn, clearly annoyed by the interruption.

"Quinn, what do you want to drink?" Austin asked.

"A club soda with a splash of cranberry juice. Thanks." She treated him to a genuine smile.

"And you, gentlemen? What would you like?" the waitress asked in a syrupy sweet voice.

They both ordered Pellegrino. Austin was keeping his body clean for the organ donation and Damon was in training.

They made small talk for a little while, Quinn holding her own on discussions of the game, plays, and positions.

After they ordered their meals, Quinn placed her napkin on the table. "If you'll both excuse me, I'll be back in a few minutes." She rose and headed for the ladies' room, and as he expected, Damon watched her go.

He waited until she was far enough away before letting out a low whistle. "Damn, bro. You should have fucked her, not hired her."

Austin narrowed his gaze. "Watch how you talk about her, asshole."

"Whoa." Damon raised his hands in a gesture of peace. "Hey, I didn't mean anything by it. Since when are you so damn sensitive about any woman?"

Austin forced himself to relax. Damon was right. Unless someone insulted the females in his family, he was usually calmer than this. Something about Quinn fired up his protective instincts, not that she needed him to look out for her. She could clearly hold her own. But he didn't like the sound of his brother demeaning her in any way.

"So she's different." Placing his hands behind his head and stretching, Damon met his gaze.

"Yeah. But she's off-limits." Austin pinned his

brother with a steady stare, making sure the kid knew he meant back off.

"Message received." Damon looked past Austin and gave a short incline of his head, letting him know Quinn had returned.

She rejoined them at the table and they had an enjoyable lunch. One where he was damned glad the tablecloth blocked the view of his dick, because everything about her did it for him. Her laugh, her stories, her expressive words, and the full pink mouth. He didn't care what color lipstick she wore, he wanted to taste her. To feel her lips around his cock.

This hiring was going to be the test of a lifetime.

*　　*　　*

Quinn had been on the job for three weeks, and Austin had been out for the last seven days following surgery. She drove up to the house where he lived. It was more like a mansion, located in an exclusive neighborhood in South Beach. She asked herself what she was doing here and the answer was simple. She wanted to reassure him she had things under control.

In the time she'd spent by Austin's side, becoming familiar with clients and learning the office, she'd discovered she liked the man she worked for. He was demanding, which she could handle, didn't put up with shit from his young clients who thought they were

God's gift to whatever sport they excelled in, and was a whiz at negotiating and putting someone in their place. She admired him and could learn a lot from watching him.

That was the professional Quinn.

Quinn the woman still had a huge crush on her employer and admired the fact that he was donating an organ to a family member. But she would never act on her feelings, and the job, as she'd hoped, was perfect for her.

Austin treated her with the utmost respect, and never in the time they'd been together had he crossed any boundaries or treated her like a woman he desired. She had, however, caught him looking at her with a slow simmer in his eyes more than once and convinced herself she was imagining things. It was for the best that they remain professional.

Needing something to hold when she walked in to face him, she'd stopped on the way and found the perfect item along with a package of Tim Tams her friend had brought home from Australia.

She headed up the long driveway filled with cars and across the walkway. The door was partially open, so she pushed the doorbell and walked inside.

Bri greeted her immediately with a warm hug. "It's so nice of you to stop by." She glanced at the bag in Quinn's hand. "Aww, you didn't have to bring the patient a gift," she said with a grin. "Come meet everyone."

Quinn followed Bri through a marble entryway into a hallway filled with people. The men all had a distinct family resemblance, not to mention the same requisite amount of testosterone. Wow, those Prescotts were hot, she mused as Bri pulled her past the guys who'd, for whatever reason, ended up in the hallway and into a big family room, where Damon sat in an oversized reclining chair drinking from a can of soda and watching television while Austin lay on the sofa.

"Your highness, you have a visitor," Bri said, causing Quinn to chuckle. Bri turned her gaze to Damon. "You. Out. Let them catch up so Austin stops asking what's going on at the office. I'll go feed the rest of the crew," she said.

Damon smirked at Austin, then headed out. Bri's voice rose as she shepherded the family into the kitchen and the din of voices grew lower.

Austin gestured for her to come farther into the room. He looked good in a pair of gray sweats and a navy tee shirt as he leaned back against a suede over-sized sofa that was located in front of the massive large screen. The beard on his face suited him, and those gorgeous indigo eyes stared at her, a slow grin forming on his sensual mouth.

"To what do I owe the pleasure?" he asked.

"I wanted to see for myself how you're doing. And here. I brought you something."

She handed him the bag, watching and suddenly embarrassed as he pulled out a stuffed horse, the Thunder mascot, wearing a jersey. "I love it," he said on a low, sexy laugh.

"I didn't want to come empty-handed."

"What's this?" He held the Tim Tams in his hand.

"You've never had Tim Tams? They're only the best Australian cookie *ever*. Chocolate biscuits surrounded by a chocolate cream filling." She moaned at the thought of the cookie she'd had this morning, remembering the taste that had exploded on her tongue.

His eyes dilated at her unintentional sexual sound. Shit. She cleared her throat. "You should try one."

An amused smile lifted his lips. "I will. And thank you, Quinn," he said in his rumbling voice. "Have a seat. I can't stand or I'd be a gentleman and do the right thing my parents taught me."

Grinning, she sat with a good amount of space between them.

"I've never seen you in jeans," he said.

She blinked in surprise. "No, I guess you haven't. But I wasn't going to come here dressed for the office."

His gaze drank her in. "Well, I like the casual look on you."

"I ... thank you."

He blinked and shook his head. "Sorry. That was inappropriate. So how have things been at the office? I've tried to check in, but my family has been alternating as babysitters, making sure I don't do much as per doctor's orders. Another five weeks of doing nothing and I may lose my mind."

She smiled, knowing how much he thrived on work. "Everything is fine. Quiet. You can relax and heal."

"Can we go over some of the new endorsements that have come in? I know Bri's helping you as is Rex King." He referred to the main agent who was directing her in Austin's absence. "But I hate being out of the loop. So show me those papers I know you slipped into your bag."

He winked at her and damned if her panties didn't grow damp. Damn, the man was potent.

She shot him a mock glare and pulled out a bunch of offers from her purse. Drawing a deep breath, she slid closer until her thigh touched his and his body heat radiated through the soft denim. She swallowed hard, doing her best to ignore his warm masculine scent that smelled so good.

He perused the documents, going over each by

athlete, giving her his opinion, and placing the finished ones on his other side. She took notes, offering her own two cents deal by deal, but she saw him fading fast. Bri had told her he'd been warned about the exhaustion part of the recovery, hence his inability to return to work for a total of six full weeks and no heavy lifting at all.

She pulled the papers out of his hand. "You need to rest."

He frowned. "Dammit. The doctors said the fatigue could last a good three months while my body gets used to filtering through one kidney."

"Well, behave yourself. Do what the doctors say and you'll be back in no time." She glanced across his lap and reached for the papers he'd put aside.

Her arm brushed the bulge in his pants and she sucked in a breath. He stiffened and grabbed her wrist with one hand. Seconds passed with just the sound of their harsh inhales and exhales echoing between them.

"Quinn," he said in a gruff voice.

She turned her head. Big mistake. Her gaze met his and his lips were way too close.

"You should move away," he said, not making an effort to shift his own head at all.

"I know," she whispered. But she was frozen in place, the desire to kiss him, to feel the beard that now covered his face against her skin overwhelming.

His grip on her wrist tightened. And still she didn't turn away. So he closed the distance between them and sealed his lips over hers. Her lashes fluttered closed and she met him halfway, accepting the kiss. His mouth slid over hers, causing her body to come alive. Flutters took up residence in her stomach, and yearning slid like honey through her veins. He might be lacking stamina but his kiss was strong enough to consume her whole.

He parted his mouth, his facial hair tickling her lips as his tongue speared inside and tangled with hers. She groaned and his free hand came up to her neck, gripping her tight and holding her in place as he continued the delicious onslaught.

If not for the recent surgery, nothing would stop her from climbing into his lap, settling herself over the hard erection that was still pressing into her arm, and grinding against him while he continued the deep, drugging kiss. His lips played with hers, their tongues tangled and teeth clashed, and she knew he wanted *more*, just as she did.

"Jesus Christ, Austin. You just had major surgery. Can't this wait?" a male voice asked.

Though Austin released his grip on her neck, he didn't seem nearly as disturbed as she was, and she jumped back, mortified.

"Calm your shit, *Dr. Prescott*. I haven't moved an

inch. No violating doctor's orders," Austin said in a desire-laden voice.

She closed her eyes, wanting the floor to swallow her whole. She peeked over and saw Braden shaking his head at his brother.

"I'm sorry." She jumped up, kneeling for the papers that fell to the floor.

"Quinn—"

Austin said her name but she ignored him, gathering the documents.

Braden stepped over and helped her. "Relax," he said in her ear. "He's perfectly fine. I'm just making sure he doesn't pull his Steri-Strips."

She shook her head. "No. This shouldn't have happened. I work for him." She stood and shoved the documents into her purse.

"Braden, give us a minute," Austin said.

His brother left the room and she forced herself to meet Austin's concerned gaze.

"I shouldn't have kissed you. If I made you uncomfortable, I'm sorry," he said.

"You didn't. Make me uncomfortable, I mean. I wanted you to kiss me. It just can't happen again. I need this job." She had student loans for what her scholarship didn't cover. Hell, given the way she was raised, taking care of every baby in her family, siblings and cousins, she needed this job to validate who she was as a person. "I love this job. And I'm not going to risk it by getting involved with my boss."

Especially not with a playboy who could pick up any woman he wanted at any random meal of the day. And she'd certainly seen females be less than circumspect, slipping him their number, rubbing against him, and being outright rude to Quinn, pushing her aside when they were out for business.

"I value you, Quinn. I don't want to lose you either."

She managed a nod.

"So we're good?" he asked.

"We're fine." Even if her body was still quivering inside from the best kiss she'd ever had.

*   *   *

Quinn left like the flames of hell were licking at her heels, and Austin didn't blame her. What the fuck was he doing, acting on his deepest desire and kissing the best assistant he'd ever had? Even in the short time she'd been working for him, he knew she could handle him. His demands. His clients. Their tantrums. He couldn't afford to lose her.

"Bro, damn, what were you thinking?" Braden sauntered into the room and slid into the chair Damon had occupied earlier.

"I wasn't," he muttered.

"Oh, you were, all right. Just with the wrong head."

Austin rolled his eyes. "Shut the fuck up," he said without heat.

He missed his brother when he was abroad, working for Doctors Without Borders, and Austin was glad he had Braden home for a brief time now.

"Holy shit, are those Tim Tams?" Braden flew out of the chair and planted his ass next to Austin, grabbing the cookies from beside him and opening them without asking.

"Hey! Those are mine."

"And you can share them unless you want me to run off with them, leaving you with none. It's not like you can chase me." Braden rolled a shoulder.

Austin shook his head. Jesus Christ. Siblings.

His brother pulled open the crinkly package and snagged a couple of biscuits, handing the rest back to Austin. "She must really like you if she gave you these."

"She works for me. What you saw was a slip. It won't happen again." *It couldn't happen again.*

His brother chuckled. "Keep telling yourself that. I saw how you two looked at each other."

"What are you, the expert on relationships now? I thought you were single."

Braden was the sibling closest in age to Austin, so

they were tight. Always had been. "Let's say there's someone with possibility." His eyes gleamed and Austin knew his brother was in deep.

"I'm happy for you. As for me, I'm going to heal and get back to playing the field. After all, it's what I do best." He would put Quinn in the off-limits zone and keep her there.

He had no other choice.

Chapter One

Quinn sashayed out of Austin Prescott's office, sweet curves encased in a tight black skirt with high fuck-me heels completing the outfit.

"Stop staring at your assistant's ass, or at the very least, don't be obvious about it."

Austin cupped the back of his neck in his hand and let out a groan.

"You're right," he said to Marcus Powers, an agent in his office and a close friend. "It's not cool." Quinn was the best executive assistant ever and Austin didn't want to lose her.

She'd proven herself to be extremely intelligent, could keep up with negotiations, handle the wise-ass players Austin represented, and on the times they went out for meals, make small talk with their fancy wives. Oh, and she tasted like the sweetest treat he'd ever had.

He knew because they'd had one slip. A slip he couldn't get out of his head, even a year later. The fireworks that had exploded between them were vivid even now. But they'd never discussed that moment again.

Quinn was a different sort of woman than the groupies who used to chase him in his NFL days. Everything about her appealed to him, but he did his best to treat her with respect. When he wasn't inadvertently staring at her ass, that is. It was dicey to have an affair with a co-worker, someone for whom he was directly in charge of her career. And she didn't strike him as a one-and-done kind of woman, and that was his MO. Not that he thought one time with Quinn would be enough.

"Are you going to Allstars tonight?" Marcus asked of the exclusive sports and cigar bar in South Beach that catered to the elite athlete.

It was a place players and industry people could frequent without groupies and hangers-on bothering them. Which wasn't to say Austin couldn't find a woman to hook up with there. Just that there was a higher class of female to choose from than a run-of-the-mill establishment.

He ran a hand over his face. Maybe hanging out with friends and possibly going home with a woman was just what he needed to take the edge off this gnawing desire for Quinn. Since he'd put his rampant playboy days behind him, he was more discriminating and discreet, yet it had still been too long since he'd gotten laid.

"Sure. I'll be there."

"Awesome." Marcus pulled out his phone to check his email.

Just then, Austin's desk phone buzzed and he picked up the receiver. "Yes?"

"You're needed in the conference room. You and Marcus both," Quinn said in her normal voice. But he even found her husky tone arousing. "Can I let your sister know you're coming?" she asked.

"Tell her we'll be right there."

Although she wasn't a full partner, Bri had a definite say in how things ran around here. If something went wrong, she sorted out the issue.

"We're wanted in the conference room. Apparently Bri's called a meeting." Austin pushed up from his chair.

"Any idea what she wants?" Marcus asked.

He shook his head. "Not a clue but we might as well go find out."

He headed for the conference room, Marcus right behind him, stepped inside, and heard, "Surprise!"

Blinking into the bright room, he realized the entire staff was present, along with his family. In the corners, gold and white balloons decorated the room, and a large cake sat on the rectangular gleaming wood table.

"What is all this?" he asked, confused. It wasn't his birthday.

Bri sidled up beside him, her long blonde hair pulled into a bun at the back of her head. "Today is one year since the kidney transplant. A year since you saved Uncle Paul's life."

Paul Dare walked up to him, looking healthy, his skin tanned, his eyes clear and gleaming. "Thank you ... son."

Everyone in this room knew the word *son* meant so much more to both than a random term of endearment. When Jesse Prescott, the man who'd raised them as his own, hadn't been able to have children, Austin's mother, Christine, had turned to her best friend since childhood to help her via sperm donation. Her gay best friend. The man she'd been in love with but couldn't have. To say it had been a shock was an understatement.

"You're welcome," Austin said to Paul, who he still called *uncle*.

Austin pulled the older man into a brief hug before releasing him. "Any chance you and Ron will come to Allstars tonight? Marcus and I are going."

"I'll be there," Bri chimed in.

"We'll try. Ron's been sick this week. I'll see if he's feeling up to it," Paul said of his long-time partner, Ron Mayburn. Another Prescott family friend who'd been loyal to them for years.

"Give him my best and don't push him if he's not up to it. And let's do dinner soon. The three of us," Austin said.

"Sounds good." Paul smiled. "So what about you? When are you going to settle down?"

Austin grimaced at the thought. "I like my life the way it is, thank you very much."

"Really? You like going home alone at night to a house that echoes because it's so big but empty? Ordering in dinner? Eating by yourself?" Paul lowered his voice so they wouldn't be overheard.

"Whoa, what is with the third degree?" Austin asked, surprised.

"I just worry about all of you. Single. Alone. Even your mother seems open to a new relationship, but you kids?" He shook his head. "I just want the best for you."

One look into his serious indigo eyes and Austin knew they were related. It was a miracle none of them had caught on sooner, but then no one ever had a reason to assume they weren't Jesse Prescott's children by blood.

"Well, trust me, I'm not always lonely." Austin winked at his uncle, unwilling to admit that just maybe the truth hit a little close to home. But not enough to consider settling down any time soon. If anything, he was now even more determined to get laid and get rid of this annoying desire for someone he couldn't admit to clawing at him inside.

"I'm always here if you need me," Paul said before turning to talk to one of the agents in the office.

Letting out a breath, Austin took a minute to just *be* before he made the rounds as well, thanking everyone for showing up for this impromptu party.

Before he could begin, Quinn came up to him, a warm smile on her beautiful face. "I know I've said it before, but you did a wonderful thing for Paul and for your family," she said, her green eyes shining with admiration.

Her approval meant something to him he couldn't quite name, but her praise also made him uncomfortable. "I just did what anyone would do." He shifted on his feet.

She shook her head, a wry smile lifting her lips. "That's what makes what you did so special. You really believe it was no big deal." She reached up and patted his cheek, obviously meaning it to be a friendly tap, but their eyes met and her touch lingered.

With her soft hand against his face, he wanted nothing more than to grab her wrist, pull her close, and kiss her ... again. Since the yearning had been building for a year, and knowing he was no longer incapacitated by surgery, their union wouldn't be soft and sweet, either.

A loud laugh broke the silence. Cheeks flushed, Quinn stepped back and turned away, walked to the table, and began cutting the cake, head down, not meeting his gaze.

Not well done of him, he thought and groaned. Time to focus on the gathering around him and his workers. He clapped his hands. "Okay, everyone, eat cake, be merry, and head home for the day. My way of showing my appreciation for the party."

That pronouncement earned him a round of applause. Even if it was already four p.m. on a Friday, leaving early was leaving early, and cutting his employees some slack was good for morale.

He waited until he'd spoken to and thanked everyone, and made certain he was the last to leave the office before heading out, locking up behind him.

Then Austin, Bri, and Marcus met up for a steak dinner. Afterwards they settled in at Allstars for a drink and well-deserved relaxation. The dark oak walls of the bar, the low sconce lighting, and the comfortable club chairs settled him.

"Hello, Austin, long time no see." Marnie, a cocktail waitress at the bar, sidled up close to him.

"Hi, yourself. How are you?" he asked.

She batted her lashes. "How do I look?" she asked flirtatiously.

He chuckled at the way she deliberately was fishing for compliments. They had history, he and Marnie, as in he'd fallen into bed with her once before.

With her auburn hair that hung long and wavy around her shoulders and a killer body, she was easy on the eyes. She didn't do it for him like a certain green-eyed assistant, but *she* was off-limits. Marnie wasn't.

He dragged his gaze up her long legs in black pants up to her silk camisole, also black. Her breasts were perky and her smile welcoming. "You look pretty damn fine from where I'm sitting," he said.

Marnie grinned, gripping her round cocktail tray in her hands. "So what can I get for you?" she asked in a husky voice.

"The usual." Actually it was his old usual as he didn't drink often since his kidney donation. But a Don Julio would sit well right now.

"And maybe a little something later? My shift ends early tonight," she offered, leaning down so he could see her lush cleavage.

Austin grinned because he'd just found his willing woman to take home for the night.

*   *   *

Quinnlyn Stone walked into Allstars with her brother, Matt, by her side. Although she'd wanted nothing more than to go home after work, he'd insisted they needed to meet and talk in person. Worried about him because she was the oldest of four siblings and it had always been her job to watch out for the others, she'd agreed but insisted on going someplace quiet. After the party at the office and being around people for an hour in a small room, she wanted some peace.

These days, crowds and loud noises made her a little anxious. She likened it to a mild form of PTSD, similar to her cousin who had been an extremely colicky baby. Even a decade later, she couldn't listen to an infant crying without being transported back to the intense feelings of failure and frustration of those days.

Allstars was on the top level of an exclusive hotel, but she waited in the lobby for her brother because it was hot and humid in Miami in August. She hadn't seen her brother in a while because he'd missed last month's Sunday dinner at her parents' house.

When he walked in, she grinned. "Matty!" She ran up and wrapped her arms around him, hugging him tight before releasing him and taking him in. His jet-black hair was combed, his glasses with black frames sat on his face, and his sport jacket was perfectly pressed. "Look at my baby brother in his college professor attire."

He chuckled but rolled his eyes. "You're twenty-eight. I'm two years younger than you. Jeffrey's the baby."

At twenty-one, yes, he was. But so was Matt. "As long as you're younger, you're the baby, so humor me."

"I am humoring you. I'm letting you bring me to a place where jocks hang out, aren't I?"

She wrinkled her nose. "That's a snobby, elitist thing to say. Now, come. Let's go have a drink and you can tell me why you wanted to see me." She clasped his hand, led him to the elevator, and hit the button for the top floor.

They walked out, and as they waited for the hostess to lead them to a table, she heard a familiar laugh that sent tingles down her spine and a jolt of pure awareness through her veins. After hearing his voice all day, she should be immune to such a typical feminine reaction. Quinn always knew when Austin Prescott was nearby.

"Your table is ready," an attractive waitress with blonde highlights in her hair said.

"Thank you." They started for the table when Quinn heard her name. "We'll be right there," she said to the other woman.

"Matt, come say hello to Austin."

"The jock boss," he said low enough that only she could hear.

"What do you have against athletes?" she asked.

The rest of the family loved sports. She came by her choice of job naturally. Her dad was a die-hard Miami Thunder fan.

"I know their social reputations. I just don't want you to end up a notch in this guy's bedpost."

Her eyes opened wide. "Oh my God, Matt! He's been nothing but professional since I started working for him." If she ignored the one kiss that consumed her dreams.

She pulled her brother over to Austin's table, where he sat with Bri and Marcus. "Matt, you've met Austin. This is his sister, Bri, who works PR at the firm, and Marcus, who is an agent. Guys, this is my brother, Matt."

They all exchanged hellos.

"I didn't know you'd be here tonight," she said to Austin, who looked casual and relaxed. His white shirt was unbuttoned, showing a smattering of chest hair she had to drag her eyes away from. And right now those gorgeous unique-colored indigo eyes were hot on her face.

"I was dragged here by these two." He gestured to the others at the table. "What brings you out tonight?"

She glanced at her sibling. "Matt wanted to talk. I figured this place was a good choice."

Austin inclined his head. "So I don't suppose I can convince you to join us?"

She smiled but shook her head. "I need to know what Matt wants."

A low laugh sounded from beside her. "I want a drink."

Quinn grinned. "And that's my cue. I'll see you Monday?" she asked.

Austin nodded. "See you Monday."

Matt grasped her hand and led her to the table the hostess had indicated earlier, and a little while later, she sat with a glass of Chardonnay, while her brother drank a scotch and soda. They talked about home, their parents, their siblings, and their jobs, catching up. But all the while, she was acutely aware of Austin. And the waitress who was definitely flirting with him in ways that couldn't be misconstrued.

Quinn ought to be used to the attention Austin garnered. From the first business lunch they'd attended, women ignored Quinn and threw themselves at Austin. He had cleavage lowered into in his face, boobs brushed against his arm, phone numbers slipped into his jacket pocket ... and she could go on. He laughed it off to being an ex-NFL star.

But in the time Quinn had been working for him, he'd been discreet. He didn't parade women in the office and never had he asked her to make a lunch or dinner reservation for a date. But the man wasn't a monk, and he clearly had no intention of settling down.

"Quinnie-Boo, God, are you even listening to me?"

She blinked when Matt snapped his fingers in front of her face and even called her by that awful childhood nickname to get her attention. "I'm sorry. I was lost in thought. But I'm paying attention now." She couldn't spend time thinking about her boss and his strong, chiseled features and tanned skin. Or the muscled body beneath the suit. She needed to stop letting her mind wander there.

"I guess you want to know why I asked to see you in person?" Matt asked.

Finally, he got to the crux of things. "I take it you didn't just want to see your sister?"

He shook his head. "I mean, of course I did, but I also wanted to tell you something." Her brother looked like he was chewing glass, that what he had to reveal was that upsetting.

"What is it?" She put her hand on his.

"I ran into Daniel at a faculty meeting on campus."

She startled at the mention of her ex-fiancé. "Oh. Okay?" She and Daniel Munroe had ended things on an awkward note.

Matt had introduced them because he and Daniel were colleagues at the smaller college where they both taught. She and Daniel had bonded over the notion that neither one of them wanted children. As the oldest of the family, she'd raised her siblings and was quite content with any nieces or nephews that might come along who she could spoil.

She'd *thought* they'd been on the same page. So when he'd asked her to marry him, it seemed like the right thing to do. They enjoyed each other's company and could each focus on their careers. Until the day he revealed he really did want kids and had assumed she'd change her mind at some point in time.

When she assured him she hadn't ... wouldn't ... he'd asked her to at least agree to reconsider things down the road. But she knew better than to go into a marriage with something as fundamental as wanting children undecided. She'd ended things and hadn't seen him over a year.

"And?" she asked into the silence.

Matt drummed his fingers against the table. "His wife is pregnant and I wanted you to hear it from me. In case you took it hard or had had second thoughts." He stared at her with love and concern in his eyes, and she adored him for it, but she did not understand her family.

Her parents thought, after helping to raise their kids and her younger cousins, she'd want to be a nanny instead of having a career, and her brother believed she'd be hurt by her ex doing exactly what he'd told her he'd wanted. Or maybe the problem was her family just didn't understand her.

"I'm fine. Why wouldn't I be? I knew Daniel wanted kids. Well, eventually I knew, although it would have been nice if he'd told me from the beginning and not assumed I'd change my mind."

She glanced at her sibling, who still looked worried. "I realized pretty quickly after we broke up that I didn't love him the way I should or I would have been a lot more upset by the end of things." She bit down on her lower lip, remembering that odd feeling of relief after things had ended.

"And by the way, same goes for him. He was engaged again within a year. It's all good, Matt, but thank you for worrying about me." She squeezed her brother's hand and he let out a relieved breath.

From the corner of her eye, she saw the waitress approach Austin once more, lean down, and whisper in his ear. Whatever she said, it was an intimate action that had nothing to do with his drink order, and he placed his hand on her waist and squeezed once in reply, causing Quinn's stomach to twist at the sight.

"Well, I'm glad to hear you're okay," her brother said, oblivious to her inner turmoil over Austin.

She forced a smile, still keeping an eye out as Austin reached inside his pants pocket for his wallet, handing the waitress his credit card. She strode off and brought the bill back for him to sign. And not five minutes later, Austin stood up, hugged his sister, shook hands with Marcus, and started for the door, meeting up with the woman who'd obviously just gotten off her shift. Together they walked out the door.

But not before Austin turned back and his gaze caught on Quinn's. She hadn't meant to continue staring. Hadn't anticipated him turning back and looking her way. Something flashed in his expression before he shuttered it and quickly jerked his head back around and headed out the door.

Quinn sighed. As much as she hated to admit it, watching Austin with another woman hurt more than breaking up with her ex had. She'd grown close to Austin while working for him and had kept that kiss they'd shared close to her heart.

Until today, she hadn't had to see him with one of his conquests, and reality was a bitter pill to swallow. The truth was, she had no business having feelings for her boss. Her job was too good to lose.

He had every right to do his thing and she'd do her own. Live and let live. And she'd move forward secure in the knowledge her heart wouldn't get broken by her playboy boss.

Chapter Two

Austin sat in his Porsche 911 Turbo with Marnie in the passenger seat. Enclosed in the small space, he was suddenly aware of the cloying scent of her perfume that would no doubt linger long after she exited the vehicle. Why hadn't he noticed that it bothered him before?

Dammit, he knew why, he thought, and curled his fingers tighter around the leather steering wheel. As he'd walked out, he'd had a compelling need to turn back around. He had. And he'd met Quinn's gaze. In her eyes, he'd seen a wounded look that seared him to his soul. Although they weren't together, he now felt uncomfortable being with Marnie, who'd merely been a substitute for the female he couldn't have.

As she reached over and placed her hand on his thigh, Austin tensed, wishing he'd made an excuse to go home alone. But he hadn't and there was no valid reason he couldn't enjoy this night. He was single, available, and dammit, he needed to get laid, and Marnie was clearly interested.

"I'm so glad you took me up on my offer," she

said, sliding her hand closer to his crotch.

Driving, he grasped her wrist and slid her fingers away from his dick, which sadly hadn't reacted the way he'd hoped once they got things going between them. Fuck. "Come on, Marnie. We'll have plenty of time back at my place. I'll make it worth the wait."

He caught her pout from the corner of his eye.

"I don't remember you being so stuffy," she said.

"I just don't want to get pulled over because your hand is on my cock and I'm swerving all over the road." He threaded his fingers through hers, keeping one hand on the wheel. "Relax and I'll make you feel good soon," he promised.

"Fine." She huffed and settled back into her seat.

He turned off at his exit and finally, after what felt like an eternity, drove into his neighborhood and up to his gated property. The house wasn't truly enclosed, the gates were just for show, ending at the lit pillars on either side of the drive. He pulled all the way up and parked, planning to walk to the front door. With a little luck, he'd be taking Marnie home afterward, so no need to take the car inside the garage.

No sooner had he turned off the ignition than she began to slide across the center console and he cleared his throat. "Lots of beds inside. Counters, too. You can take your pick." Looking at her, he winked, hoping she took his words as charming and not the blow off he was giving her.

This was going to be a long fucking ordeal. Too bad men couldn't claim headaches and call it a night.

"Jeez." She unsnapped her seat belt and opened her door.

He met her outside the car and wrapped an arm around her waist in an effort to calm her down by pulling her against him. "It's going to be good." He gave her ass a squeeze and she giggled, allowing him to relax.

In the distance, a strange noise captured his attention. "Did you hear that?" he asked.

She shook her head but then the noise sounded again. "Yes. Is that ... a cat? A kitten?" She moved more quickly toward the front door and the sound, which was becoming louder and more persistent.

He shrugged and rushed after her. The front porch lights shone down on the steps, and he realized something had been left outside the double doors, his stomach churning at the sight.

Marnie stopped in her tracks. "That's a baby carrier."

He blinked to clear his vision because he'd really hoped he'd been wrong, that he hadn't seen *that*. "I'm sorry, *say that again*?" Because he had to be sure. He was suddenly too queasy to be thinking rationally.

"It's a baby carrier and that noise is a baby!"

Marnie's voice rose in panic.

"What the fuck?" Hesitantly, he took the three steps and looked at the car seat he'd seen his friends with kids use.

Movement came from inside, and as he bent down, two blue eyes stared up at him, and he noticed what looked like a pink sticky note stuck to the shifting blanket.

Frowning, he bent down and retrieved the note with three words scrawled onto it.

Jenny is yours.

His stomach churned and he'd be lucky if he didn't lose what was left in his stomach.

"Holy fuck, Austin! You have a kid!" Marnie said, obviously reading over his shoulder and now sounding hysterical.

And at her panicked shriek, the baby began to cry, loud wails that traumatized him immediately because he didn't know what the fuck to do.

"Pick her up!" he shouted over the din.

Eyes wide, Marnie shook her head. "Hell no. That wasn't part of tonight's deal." She'd already grabbed her phone and begun tapping on the screen.

"What are you doing?" he asked, his gaze darting between the woman he'd hoped would take charge and the infant who'd thrown off the white blanket that had covered her. Little legs covered in footed pajamas now kicked up a storm as the screams she let out increased in volume.

"I'm calling an Uber. What do you think I'm doing?" Marnie looked as panicked as he felt.

Desperate, he grabbed her wrist. "Please, don't go. Stay. Help me."

She shook her head. "Oh, no. I'm meeting the car at the end of the driveway. Good luck, Austin. You're on your own." With that pronouncement, she and her high heels headed down the path and away from him and this bundle of joy as fast as she could go.

He glanced again at the baby screaming her little lungs out. Thank God it was warm out, but maybe too warm, and he picked up the carrier handle in one hand, the bag he'd just noticed in the other, and brought the infant inside the air-conditioned house. He took the baby into the kitchen and settled the carrier on the floor along with what he hoped was a diaper bag. Because Lord knew he had nothing with which to feed a baby. Change a baby. Nausea threatened.

"Jesus Christ," he muttered under his breath.

The screams continued but he was scared shitless to take the baby out of the carrier and hold her.

Who could he call? His mother? He immediately discounted that idea. Before he knew what this fucking situation really was, he wasn't telling his mother someone left his baby on the doorstep.

Was it his baby? Fuck.

He ran a hand through his hair. Should he call Bri? He shook his head. His sister would be all over him about how he couldn't keep his dick in his pants, and though that had once been true, he hadn't had sex all that often in the last ... how old was this baby, anyway? At a glance, he hadn't a clue.

He paced the floor, his heart pounding as loud as the screams. He needed someone who could handle a crisis. Who wouldn't panic. Who would take charge and make him feel like everything was going to be okay.

The name of that person came to him immediately, and though he cringed at the thought of dialing her number, he really had no choice. He was desperate, at a complete and utter loss, and she was the one person he trusted to handle things. Even if it changed how she looked at him forever.

* * *

Quinn washed up, changed into a pair of sweats and a tee shirt, and climbed into bed, letting her muscles relax as she settled against her fluffy pillows. Instead of thinking about her night, which would only lead to her remembering moments she didn't want to dwell on, like Austin leaving with that woman or her family's lack of understanding her, she picked up her Kindle to dive into a romantic comedy she'd been reading. Once she chilled out enough, she'd shut the light and try to fall asleep.

No sooner had she begun reading than her phone rang.

A glance told it was Austin and her heart began to race. What could he want this late? Something had to be wrong and she grabbed the phone, answering immediately. "Hello?"

"I need you. Really, desperately need you. Can you get over to my place now?"

In the background, she heard an indistinguishable sound. "What is it? What's wrong?" she asked, knowing he'd left with the waitress, or at least she thought he had.

"Just get over here fast. Please." He disconnected the call, leaving her staring at the phone in her hand.

Worried now, she glanced down at her outfit, decided it was good enough given the strange circumstances, grabbed her car keys, and rushed out the door. At this time of night, there was little traffic on the roads, and she arrived at Austin's house in less than twenty minutes, pulled into his driveway, and parked behind his Porsche.

She rushed to the front door, finding it open, which was odd, stepped inside, and loud baby screams assaulted her senses. She immediately thought she was dreaming. Austin had an infant in his house? How could that be?

She walked through the main entryway with gorgeous vibrant paintings on the walls and toward the too familiar sound. She knew the way. Not only had she been here after Austin's surgery but she'd dropped contracts and paperwork off on occasional days he'd been sick or working from home, so she headed toward the kitchen.

"Austin?" she called over the angry, upset sounds.

"In here!" he yelled back.

She stepped inside and froze.

He stood over a baby in a car seat carrier, literally wringing his hands.

"What's going on?" she asked.

"Someone left her on my doorstep!"

Quinn immediately bent down and shifted the handle so she could lift the crying infant out of the seat and cuddle her against her chest. "Shh. Shh."

She rocked from side to side, rubbing her hand over the little back in a soothing motion. "What's in that bag? See if there's formula or diapers." Something that would soothe the baby.

But as he knelt, the infant responded to being comforted and held by Quinn. The baby calmed down and pulled in quick breaths, then released them.

"Oh, thank God. She stopped crying. How did you do that?" Austin asked, glancing up from his crouched position.

"You were a tense mess and transmitting that to her. Plus you didn't pick her up or even try and comfort her," Quinn chided him.

"She scares me. I don't know shit about babies." He dug through the bag on the floor. "What's this?" He held up a burp rag.

Quinn rolled her eyes. "Give it to me." She took the soft cotton and dabbed at the little one's wet face and eyes and wiped her tiny nose. "There you go. All better?" she asked.

Two big blue eyes stared up at Quinn. My God, this baby was beautiful. "You said *she*?"

He rose. "The note said she's a girl." He picked up the pink sticky note that had fallen to the floor. "Here."

She glanced at the paper and her eyes opened wide. "And you didn't know about her?" she asked, voice rising in disbelief.

"*No*," he replied a bit sheepishly.

With a frown for him, she looked back to the baby and smiled. "Hey, Jenny. You're so pretty. Are you sure she's yours?" she asked Austin, still rocking the baby in what was a natural motion that quickly came back to her from taking care of her youngest siblings and cousins.

"I don't know," he admitted.

She shot him an incredulous glance. How could he not know he had a child? "Jesus, Austin. Are you that much of a man-whore?"

He actually looked insulted. "Hey, I'm not a man-whore. Anymore," he muttered. "The last time I was with a woman was…" He paused as he obviously mentally did the math. "About a year ago. A little before surgery…"

"You mean before tonight. The last time you were with a woman before tonight was a year ago." Her voice trailed off. "Seriously?"

He nodded. "I've been busy building the business. And for the record, I wasn't with Marnie tonight," he muttered.

But they both knew if not for the baby cockblocker in her arms, he would have been.

"Didn't you leave with her?" she asked.

He nodded, not meeting her gaze. "She took one look at the baby and bolted."

"Nice." Quinn didn't try to hide her sarcasm, then bit the inside of her cheek. "Why did you call me?"

His warm gaze settled on hers. "Because you're you. You handle things. You keep me organized and settled."

"In business," she said through gritted teeth. "Why

not call your mother or sister?"

"Are you kidding?" He dipped his head. "My mother would be all gaga-goo-goo over the baby and want to keep her forever, and my sister would be all over me … well, for exactly the things you just called me out on. And I wasn't about to explain myself to my little sister."

"She's only two years younger than you but point taken." For now. There was no way this infant was becoming Quinn's problem. "Why don't you hold her and I'll check for necessities for tonight. A bottle, formula, and diapers."

A look of horror crossed his face. "I can't hold her."

"You can and you will." She handed the baby to him, giving him no choice.

He took her awkwardly into his arms and the screaming started again immediately. "See?"

Quinn adjusted the way he held Jenny so the baby felt more secure in his arms, but the cries didn't abate.

Ignoring them the best she could, she lifted the bag to the kitchen table and went through it, doing a mental inventory as she laid out each item. "Powdered formula, four diapers, a onesie, you have the burp rag, and a pacifier. Thank God. You'll be okay until morning."

Quinn picked up the pacifier and walked to the

sink, running it under the instant hot water to sterilize it, then dabbed it against her hand, waiting until the rubber cooled off. Returning to a still clearly panicked Austin, Quinn put the pacifier into the baby's mouth.

Jenny immediately sucked it right in and quieted. Until she glanced at Austin and wound up to wail once more.

"Take her, please." Austin held out the infant, her little legs dangling beneath her.

"Fine." Quinn accepted the baby and cuddled her against her chest again.

When Jenny immediately settled, Austin's shoulders relaxed. "I'm calling you the baby whisperer," he muttered.

"Let's sit down and talk," Quinn suggested.

He nodded and she followed him into his comfortable family room and the place of their kiss. Any time she walked into this room, the memory assaulted her and she was reminded that the kiss had turned her life upside down. She hadn't been with any man since.

Instead of sitting down, she kept rocking from side to side with the baby in her arms. "Think. Could she be yours?"

He threaded his hands through his hair, messing up the longer strands and giving himself an adorably shaggy look. Add the more than five-o'clock shadow and he was one sexy man.

"How old is she? I can't tell," he said.

Quinn looked at the baby's face, gauged her size, "About three months? Four? It's hard to know. I can check the size of her clothes but that's my best guess."

He groaned. "So if you do the math, nine months of pregnancy, three to four months old ... yeah, it's possible. But I wore a fucking condom. I *always* do."

She closed her eyes, not wanting to think about him with a female in an intimate situation. Not at all. "Okay, well, you'll get that sorted out. In the meantime, as I said, you're good for the night. I can make a bottle before I go so you can feed her before bed." She bent down and put the quiet baby into his arms.

"Wait, what? Where are you going? You can't leave me!" he practically yelled.

Predictably, between his loud voice and tense body, Jenny started to wail once more.

Quinn narrowed her gaze at him. "I'm going to make a bottle and you are going to learn to hold her."

"You can't leave me."

She stared at him in disbelief. "You don't expect me to move in and play nanny for you, do you?"

He treated her to his most endearing grin.

She folded her arms across her chest defensively. "Charm isn't going to work."

"What about begging? Will that work? A raise? A promotion?" he rambled, his nerves clear. So was the abject fear in his eyes and panic in his expression.

She narrowed her gaze. "I'm already your executive assistant. I can't become your executive executive assistant."

He let out a breath and glanced at the little girl in his arms. Despite his terror, there was something endearing about the man and the baby. She couldn't say no to him on a normal day but now?

Fine. She'd stay tonight and they'd figure something out in the morning. But she didn't have to let him off the hook that easily. He needed to learn to stay calm with the baby and that wouldn't happen if she kept giving in to him immediately.

"Try calming her down. I'm going to make a bottle. We'll discuss the rest when I get back."

*　*　*

An hour after Austin had called Quinn for help, she'd had baby Jenny fed, changed, burped, and settled on a nest of blankets surrounded by couch pillows beside his bed. While his head was still spinning, Quinn had stepped up and taken charge.

Watching her with the baby had been a revelation. He'd been kidding when he called her the baby whisperer, but no joke, the woman had a magic touch.

He owed her more than he could repay and was so damned grateful. For the first time since finding a baby on his doorstep, he could breathe.

"She's asleep," Quinn said softly and gestured her head toward the bedroom door.

He followed her out and, once in the hall, leaned against the wall. "Thank you."

"You're welcome. She's a sweet little thing."

"When she isn't a crying banshee," he said wryly.

Quinn treated him to a tired smile. "Unless she's colicky, babies cry when they're hungry, wet, uncomfortable, or want to be held. Relax more around her and it should help."

"I'll try."

"You do that." She chuckled. "Okay well…"

They hadn't discussed her staying the night again, and his heart sped up at the thought that she might leave him alone with the baby.

Reaching out, he grabbed her hand, and despite the baby situation, touching her sent a jolt of awareness through him. "You're staying, right?" He heard the pathetic plea in his tone and he didn't care. "Please?" When it came to this situation, he was not above begging.

She bit down on her full bottom lip, drawing his attention to her lush mouth. "I could come back in the morning."

"What if she wakes up? You see how much she hates me."

Quinn shook her head, her grin adorable. "She doesn't hate you. She's reacting to how tense you are."

"Please? I'll pay you."

"It's not about money!"

He wondered what it was about, because she was clearly good with babies. True, he was asking her to do something outside of her job description, but it wasn't illegal, for Christ sake. "If not money, then what?"

She crossed her arms over her chest. "I'll stay the night but tomorrow we are figuring out an alternate plan."

He noted she hadn't explained her own panic over helping with the infant. Instead of calling her on it, he held up his hands in agreement. "Fine. Perfect. Thank you." He blew out a sigh of relief.

"I'm assuming this huge house has a guest room?" She began to yawn and lifted a hand to cover her mouth.

He wanted her in his bed. Next to the baby and beside him, but he knew better than to push for the impossible. Any sexual feelings he had for her needed to take a back seat to his new reality.

"Sure. Come on. You can stay in the room right across the hall." Where she could be on her feet and rush to the baby when she woke up.

His house was a six-bedroom on the bay with stunning views and was a good tax write-off. Did he need a mansion? No. But he had a big family and liked the idea of being away from the hustle and bustle of downtown.

He led her to the guest room with a queen-size bed. "You have your own bathroom. There are towels, a toothbrush, toothpaste, and all the basics. My family likes to crash here every so often, so my housekeeper keeps things stocked for them." He gestured for her to go inside.

"Thank you." As she stepped past him, he caught a whiff of her perfume. He'd trained himself to ignore the sensual scent at the office, but this was his home. And with her hair up in a messy bun, wearing comfortable sweats and a tight tee shirt that showed her generous breasts, ignoring her was all but impossible.

"Get some sleep," she said, breaking into his thoughts. "Who knows how quickly we'll be woken up again."

He nodded. "Thank you, Quinn. You'll never know how much I appreciate your help."

She smiled. "You're welcome."

He walked out and headed back to his room, pausing at the sight of the infant snuggled on the pallet on the floor. His stomach twisted anew.

Sitting down on his bed, he pulled out his calendar and went back one year, scrolling through various days and weeks, and then it hit him. He'd been in Chicago a year ago, doing business with a client, and he'd been at the hotel bar. A woman had sat down beside him. Nelle Jamieson was her name. They'd flirted. She'd taken him out of his head. Given he'd recently learned about Jesse not being his real dad, he'd been in a mood, feeling alone, and they'd gone upstairs to his room.

He was a free agent. Why not? But he'd used condoms, dammit. He always used protection. Which wasn't effective if this little one was his.

He'd seen her eyes. They were a deep blue. Could get darker, turn the indigo of his family. Not that they all had that color eyes, but the gene was a strong one. Of course, he'd have a DNA test run. And he had cameras outside. He'd have to run the tape and see if he could get a good look at who'd left the baby on his front porch.

Which begged another question. What kind of woman left a defenseless, innocent baby outside at night? Alone? His protective instincts rose for this sweet baby.

He ran a hand over his face and lay down on the bed. Little noises reached his ears. He heard every move and sigh the baby made. And if she really was his, the woman who abandoned her could be damn sure she'd never get near the infant again.

Chapter Three

A scream jolted Quinn awake. Heart pounding, she rushed to the baby, instinct driving her because it had been forever since she'd had to jump up in the middle of the night to care for an infant. But her body remembered what to do before her brain even kicked into gear.

She knelt down to pick up the baby, rising and bumping into Austin's hard body.

"Shit," he muttered. "Sorry. I was just rushing on autopilot. I'm not used to this."

"Yeah, well, join the club." She adjusted the crying infant in her arms and patted her back, shifting from foot to foot in a rocking motion that soothed the baby. Her cries quieted to little sniffles. "Can you get the light?"

He stepped away, and a few seconds later, the room was bathed in brightness.

She blinked into the glare, her eyes adjusting from darkness, and when she focused, she was looking at Austin dressed in boxer briefs and nothing more, the outline of his cock and the obvious bulge in his boxers completely visible. And what a nice-size one it was. Her body reacted immediately, her nipples hardening beneath her light camisole. Dammit.

"For God's sake, put on some clothes," she snapped at him.

"Says the woman in a silk top and nothing more," he drawled in a way-too-sexy voice.

She frowned at him, realizing that while she'd been staring at him, he'd ogled right back. "I have underwear on," she muttered, grateful the baby covered her chest. "I'll change Jenny. Then I'll make a bottle. You stick close, watch, and learn." He needed to become comfortable and competent with the infant for as long as Jenny stayed with him and, assuming she was his, for the duration.

"Okay."

After Quinn diapered the baby on the pallet on the floor, giving Austin instructions, feeling his nervous, stiff body behind her, she stood up and held Jenny out to him. "Take her and let's go downstairs for the bottle."

He visibly swallowed hard and accepted the bundle.

No sooner had Quinn given him the quiet baby and he pulled her into him than she burst into tears. "She hates me," he said in a loud voice.

"Relax your body and rub her back to calm her. I

keep explaining she's reacting to your tension." She met his gaze. "You've got this, Austin. I promise. Now come on. She's hungry."

She led him to the kitchen and taught him how to make a bottle with the powdered formula that had been left in the diaper bag and heat it up correctly. For a man who had memorized football plays, he ought to have no problem remembering her directions.

"Where do you want to give her the bottle?" she asked.

He blinked in surprise. "I assumed you'd do it." He grinned. "Please?"

She chuckled and shook her head. "You've got to learn, Daddy."

His eyes opened wide at that comment.

"Come on. We'll get you set up in the bed. That way you can easily get her back to sleep without jostling her up the stairs." She didn't mention how sexy he'd look lying against the pillows with a baby in his arms.

And when he settled in and was giving Jenny her bottle, even her cynical ovaries did a little dance at the sight.

"Have a seat." He gestured to the other side of the bed.

Wary but willing, she drew a deep breath, walked around the mattress, and settled beside him, lifting her legs so she could relax. It didn't escape her notice that she was lying in Austin's bed, in his room, both barely dressed. The baby between them was the only thing that kept her sane and prevented her from crossing that invisible middle line and falling into his arms.

The fact was, they might not admit to or acknowledge the attraction, but she knew it was mutual. As he fed Jenny in silence, her eyes grew heavy. It had been a long day, first work, then drinks with her brother, and then the baby surprise. She'd never done well being woken out of a deep sleep, and she had a difficult time keeping herself awake.

*   *   *

Austin was aware of Quinn beside him in bed, attuned to every breath she took. So when she started to get sleepy, her head jerking every time she tried to wake herself, he knew it was only a matter of time before she passed out. She needed rest, and he didn't want to risk waking her to move to her room and maybe have a difficult time falling back to sleep.

Oh, who was he kidding? He wanted her beside him in his bed.

He glanced down at the baby. To his surprise, giving her a bottle wasn't difficult. Jenny did all the work, her little lips pulling on the nipple as she drank her formula. When she finished, he did as Quinn had showed him, putting the burp rag over his shoulder, laying Jenny against it, and patted her back. It wasn't long before the little thing let out a belch to rival him and his brothers during burping contests while growing up.

"That's a good girl," he said softly.

Rising slowly so as not to disturb Quinn or upset a quiet and full Jenny, he walked over to the pallet they'd created and laid her down. Still afraid to wake her and hear the screams, he tiptoed back to bed. He climbed on top of his covers and looked over at Quinn.

Her hair spread across the pillow, a few stray strands lay over her cheek, and her dark eyelashes appeared soft against her skin. Reaching over, he gently brushed the hair away from her face, and she didn't flinch or move. Exhaustion had really claimed her, so he leaned over his other side, shut the lamp, and settled on top of the covers, too, to sleep.

*　　*　　*

Sometime during the night, Quinn must have rolled over, because Austin woke up to find a soft woman in his arms. They were on his side of the bed, her body plastered to his. Her breasts rubbed against his side, her arm was wrapped across his chest, and one leg hooked over his so the warmth of her pussy pulsed against his thigh.

And his cock responded in kind, which meant now he had a hard-on and the woman he desired exactly where he wanted her. If only he could wake her with a deep, hard kiss, his tongue in her mouth or her sex, he wasn't fussy. He needed to taste her everywhere. As he lay on his back, tortured in the best possible way, debating whether or not to take that step, Quinn moaned in her sleep. He held his breath, wondering if she'd wake up and freak out to find herself in such a delicate position.

She shifted a little and moaned again, the sound completely erotic to his ears, and when she started to grind against his thigh, he thought his head would explode. Both of them.

Gritting his teeth, he knew he had to wake her. "Quinn," he whispered.

"Mmm." Her hand slid across his chest, palm splayed wide, her touch branding him.

"Quinn, wake up," he said a little louder.

"What?" She lifted her head and looked right into his eyes. "Austin?" She blinked the fuzziness of sleep away, and with awareness came a flush to her cheeks.

"Oh my God. I must have cuddled up to you in my sleep. I'm sorry." She started to shift her leg off him at the same time he began to move away, but instead of parting ways, she ended up pressing harder against him and she let out a sigh of pleasure.

They both froze.

"Austin," she whispered, her pussy arching into his thigh harder than before. She licked her lips, and he knew she didn't mean for it to be provocative but it was.

He slid his fingers into her soft, silky hair and cupped the back of her neck, tipping her head upward. So easily. He could pull her to him so easily and his lips would be on hers in an instant. But knowing she worked for him, *she* needed to ask. He couldn't initiate nor could he take.

So he waited.

She stared at him, and he could read the turmoil crossing her pretty face. He could also see the minute she came to a decision, the determination etching her features obvious.

"Kiss me, Austin." Her voice came out in a husky whisper that went straight to his already hard cock, and his grip on her scalp tightened.

Her eyes dilated with need, but he remained still because he was holding on by a thread, and if she let him off leash, he didn't want any regrets later. He needed her to be sure she didn't want to end this now before they went any further.

Before he could ask her, she pushed herself up and her lips locked with his. That was all the permission he needed. He speared his tongue between her lips, his kiss demanding and all consuming. He finally had this woman where he wanted her and he intended to make the most of it.

Flipping her onto her back, he dominated both her and the kiss, his mouth sliding over hers, teeth nipping her bottom lip, his tongue thrusting hard and deep. And with his cock, he began to grind himself in the sweet vee between her thighs. Her hands came to his hair, her fingers threaded into the longer strands and pulled at him while he made himself at home on top of her. She was pliant and willing but gave as good as she got, kissing back with the same fervor he felt for her.

His cock poised at her sex, her thin panties and his boxer briefs the only things keeping him sane, he thrust against her, swallowing every moan and pant she offered him. His cock rubbed her clit, and her hips rocked back and forth as she arched her back, grinding her pussy against him. Suddenly she stilled as she came, crying out, a sound he swallowed with his mouth but one he'd never forget.

He'd jerk off to the memory in the days to come, that much he knew.

He rolled off her and onto his side, propping his head in one hand, ignoring the aching in his cock.

Her gaze met his, still hazy with satisfaction. "We really crossed a line," she murmured.

"One we put in place. It's not like we're violating any office policy." He ran his finger down her nose and smiled. "You're pretty after you come."

She blushed even more. "Austin," she said on a groan.

"Let's not overanalyze, okay? It was mutual."

"Except you didn't—"

He shook his head. "Doesn't mean I didn't enjoy." They were speaking quietly, both aware of the baby sleeping on the floor.

Before they could continue the conversation, Jenny made her presence known, letting out a cry that Austin recognized would soon turn to a full-on fit. Enough time had passed since her last bottle that she was probably hungry.

"Do you want diaper or bottle?" he asked Quinn, feeling as if he was building a routine for Jenny. One that included Quinn.

What would happen between *them* remained to be seen.

*   *   *

With Jenny sleeping in her baby carrier in the kitchen, Austin sipped his coffee and thought about last night. He'd managed another two hours of sleep before they woke for the day. After the bottle and diaper change, Quinn had insisted on returning to her bedroom to sleep, and Austin hadn't argued, understanding she needed her space.

He did, too. He couldn't remember the last time he'd fooled around with a woman that didn't end in sex and mutual satisfaction. What he'd done with Quinn had been with her pleasure only in mind. That was extremely unlike him, and he didn't understand why everything with Quinn felt so different. So important.

This morning, they had been cordial to each other, but she'd definitely been distant around him. They'd taken turns showering, and he'd lent her a pair of sweats and a tee shirt, the smallest he could find in his drawers, and as she entered the kitchen, he realized now he had to look at her wearing his clothes.

Her damp hair hung down her shoulders, and though she wasn't petite, the outfit swallowed her body, making him jealous. He wished his arms were wrapped around her again, the way the soft cotton clung to her frame.

"So I was thinking," she said, unaware of the direction of his thoughts. "You need a ton of things from the store for the baby, and because you don't have a car seat, we can't both go shopping."

"I'll go," he said, offering quickly before she could suggest he stay home with the infant. As soon as Jenny opened her eyes, she'd take one look at him and scream until Quinn returned. He was getting used to the pattern of behavior, though admittedly, it was starting to make him feel bad.

She grinned. "I figured you'd say that, so I made a list and emailed it to your phone. You should go to Target. They'll probably have everything you need, though I have to warn you, it's a pretty extensive list because I'm assuming you're going to have Jenny for a while."

He tried to swallow but his mouth had grown dry. "I plan on calling my lawyer to set up a paternity test. And I'll check the cameras to see if I recognize who dropped her off last night, and give the tape to a PI."

Quinn walked to the coffeemaker, took the mug he'd left out for her, and poured herself a cup of coffee. "But you do plan on keeping her until you find out the results? Or will you call the authorities and turn her over to the state?"

"Fuck no!" He'd never even considered it. He might not know a damn thing about babies, but the thought of giving the screaming banshee to strangers didn't sit right with him.

When Quinn turned to face him, she had a knowing, pleased smile on her pretty face. Even without makeup, she was beautiful.

"I assumed that was the case." She chuckled. "Is there milk in the refrigerator?"

He nodded and she walked over, opened the door, and pulled out a carton, pouring a generous amount into her coffee before returning the milk to the fridge.

"So as I was saying, it's a big list. Your Porsche isn't going to hold everything." Quinn leaned against the granite countertop.

"I'll take the Navigator." He had the truck in the garage.

"Okay, good." She took a long sip of caffeine and moaned her approval, the sound reminding him of the noises she'd made when she climaxed beneath him. "Mmmm. I needed this," she said.

He needed *her*, but he had to focus on the situation and immediately realized he'd just assumed she didn't have plans today. "Do you mind staying with Jenny while I shop?" He refused to think of what he'd do when Quinn finally had to leave.

She shook her head. "I was going to do laundry and relax today. It's fine for me to stay, but on that note, don't you think you need to line up help?"

"Like who?" he asked, playing dumb. The longer he could avoid the situation the better.

"Your mother? Sister? A brother or two?" Quinn raised an eyebrow over the mug as she drank.

"I'd really rather not," he admitted, the thought of telling his family he'd possibly fathered a baby with a one-night stand not appealing.

She sighed. "I'm sure you don't expect me to move in and take care of the baby, so what's your plan?"

Actually the thought of her moving in didn't sound so bad. Jenny responded to Quinn, always settling down when Quinn held her. And if he put their sexual incident aside, because he couldn't let that count in his thought process, having Quinn around hadn't been bad at all. He liked her in his home. And the look of her in that camisole last night, her long, tanned legs peeking out from beneath the short top? Yeah, that was a sight he could get used to.

"Austin? What's your plan?" Quinn asked again.

He shrugged. "Frankly, I don't have one."

"Right. So I'll call Bri and ask her to set up a family meeting this afternoon. Suck it up because you need them."

He shuddered but knew he had no choice.

A little while later, he'd left Quinn and Jenny at the house and was headed toward Target, using the time to make some calls. Like Quinn, his attorney asked if Austin wanted him to call Child Protective Services or the authorities about the baby, and he'd immediately rejected the idea. There was a chance Jenny was his, and he wasn't putting her or any baby into the system before knowing for certain.

At Target, chaos ensued. Even with Quinn's list, Austin was at a loss. Diaper sizes were confusing as fuck. Formula, he had the exact type, but he had no idea how many cans or tubs of the stuff to purchase.

"Baby bathtub? What the fuck?"

"Excuse me, but language?" a female voice said.

He turned to see a woman with a young child in the front seat of the shopping cart. "Sorry," he muttered and changed directions, heading to the aisle with plastic bathtubs.

Another glance at the list and he groaned. Digital thermometer, changing pads, baby wipes, Diaper Genie, Balmex, infant Tylenol, baby shampoo, blankets, burp rags, bottles, nipples ... nipples? *Jesus fuck.*

He kept that inside this time. Bouncy seat, baby carrier because apparently Quinn thought he was going to strap Jenny to his chest and walk around with her dangling from his body, onesies size six-to-nine months, and pacifiers.

He drew a calming breath as he dumped everything into his cart, asking when he needed help, which was often.

He glanced at his phone to see what was next. Baby washcloths and towels. They couldn't use regular ones? Then he saw the little teddy bear towels with hoodies attached, chuckled, and bought four because why not? It meant less laundry. It was bad enough he was going to have to explain things to his housekeeper.

And Dreft.

What was Dreft? After asking a sales associate, he discovered it was hypoallergenic baby laundry detergent. How the hell did Quinn know all this stuff?

Finally he came to the last item, a car seat. He realized she'd left a stroller off the list, noticing because there was an entire aisle of the things, and he assumed it was because she wasn't sure he'd take Jenny out. But maybe the baby would like being pushed in one, so he asked the sales associate for the best stroller on the market.

Thirty minutes at checkout and a small fortune later, a young guy helped Austin bring his second cart out to the car and load everything into the back.

He headed home, breathing a sigh of relief that the shopping ordeal was over. Except when he arrived, the driveway was full of familiar cars, and that's when he remembered.

Family meeting, he thought and braced himself for the fallout.

* * *

Quinn had held her breath until Austin left to go shopping. She'd spent the last two hours in the guest bedroom tossing and turning, wondering how she'd ended up in his arms and coming apart beneath that hard, hot body.

Kiss me. She couldn't claim she hadn't been fully aware of what she was doing despite the cloud of sleepiness that had still consumed her when she'd woken up breathing in his masculine scent.

Okay, she'd made a mistake. One she wouldn't repeat. And considering he'd said not to overthink things, clearly he didn't take it all that seriously, either. Why would he? Women flocked to him, and she just wished she hadn't fallen in line as easily as the others.

She blew out a long breath just as a familiar scream sounded from the carrier. She had to admit, hearing Jenny cry didn't instill the fear in her she usually felt when she heard babies' hysteria. The tiny girl was quickly endearing herself to Quinn. She was good, only crying for things she needed, which told Quinn she'd been well cared for before being dropped off here.

On the one hand, of course that made her happy. On the other hand, she wanted reasons for Austin to be able to keep this infant if she turned out to be his. Quinn supposed abandoning the baby in the middle of the night in the heat of the summer qualified as a good reason to give the father custody.

Quinn checked the diaper, which wasn't ready for a change, and picked the baby up, lifting her out of the carrier.

"Hello, little miss." She walked around with Jenny

in her arms, talking to her while she bounced her gently. Eventually Quinn put her into the carrier and continued chatting to her while she prepared a bottle.

"You do know if Austin's your daddy, you're a very lucky girl. Once he gets the hang of things," she said as she put the powder into the bottle.

The baby gurgled, and a few minutes later, bottle made, Quinn settled into the couch in the big family room and popped the nipple into the baby's adorable puckering lips.

While Quinn fed Jenny, memories of her days doing the same thing for her family members came back to her, her younger cousins especially, and she remembered that there were times she really had enjoyed taking care of them. Like now when this sweet girl chugged her bottle as fast as she could, looking up at Quinn with wide eyes. Eyes that reminded her very much of her good-looking daddy's.

She shook her head and let the baby finish, burped and changed her, and waited for Austin's family to descend en masse.

A little while later, the doorbell rang, and still holding the baby because she'd been crying earlier, Quinn answered, catching sight of Bri on the other side.

Drawing a deep breath, she let the other woman in.

"What's the emerg ... en ... cy?" Bri's voice trailed

off as she zeroed in on the infant in Quinn's arms. "What the fuck is that?" She shook her head, her gaze never leaving Jenny. "Never mind. I know it's a baby but what's it doing here?"

Bri stepped inside and Quinn closed the door. "I think that's your brother's story to tell, but isn't she cute?" She turned the baby to face Bri, who looked at the infant, eyes huge.

"Is she—?"

"Nope," Quinn cut off Bri's question. "Not answering." Explaining the situation was definitely Austin's job.

Bri frowned, obviously not liking being in the dark. "Okay, then what are *you* doing here with the baby?"

Quinn sighed and readjusted Jenny against her. "Austin called me and that's all I'm going to say. Come in. Is the rest of the family on their way?"

Bri nodded. "Mom should be here any minute. Damon's in town so he's coming," she said of their youngest sibling, who played football for Ian's team, the Miami Thunder. "Jaxon is between games so he's coming, too."

The baseball player brother, Quinn thought.

"And of course, Braden is halfway around the world with Doctors Without Borders," Bri said of her twin. She sighed at that.

"You miss him, don't you?" Quinn had heard the

twins were close.

She nodded. "It's hard when he's not always available to talk."

"I get it. I'm close with my siblings, too. Not that I have a twin. I'm sure that bond is different."

Bri smiled. "It is."

"Well, come on in. Coffee's available. Your brother only has a single-cup brewer, but I'll make you some." Quinn turned and started for the kitchen, Bri right behind her.

"Thanks but I can make my own. You're his business assistant not his housekeeper," Bri said, shooting her a knowing look. One that said she was very at home in Austin's house.

Quinn refused to think too hard about that and settled the now quiet baby into the carrier as the doorbell rang again. "I'll go let them in. Can you keep an eye on the baby?" she asked Bri.

Austin's sister nodded but she narrowed her gaze. "I don't like not being in the loop."

Quinn chuckled. "All will be revealed in due time," she said and headed to let the other family members in.

*   *   *

Pulling in a calming breath, Austin let himself into his house, braced for whatever reaction his family had to his supposed baby. He felt bad that he hadn't gotten back in time to do the explaining, but Quinn was more than capable of handling his family. He left the truck in the garage, planning to get his brothers' help unloading the packages.

"Hello!" he called out.

"In the family room," Damon yelled back.

"And you have some explaining to do." That was Bri.

He groaned and walked into the room. As expected, his family began shouting questions at him the second they saw him.

His mother walked up to him. Not surprisingly, Jenny was in her arms. His mother loved babies. She constantly hounded her kids to get married and give her grandchildren, and Austin wondered if she'd gotten her wish.

Her concerned gaze rested on his. Always put together, her blondish-brown hair hanging to her shoulders, her makeup fresh, Christine Prescott was special. And she was an amazing mother. She'd done her best to protect her kids from their father, Jesse, when he was in one of his moods. Over the top with his expectations. If she had one flaw, it had been that she hadn't left her husband, but she'd loved him and kept hoping her influence would fix things.

"Is she yours?" his mother asked, rubbing Jenny's

back as she spoke.

His siblings grew silent as they waited for his answer.

Austin swallowed hard, surprised Quinn hadn't revealed what little they knew about the baby, and he met Quinn's gaze, the unspoken question obvious.

She looked at him with sympathy in her eyes. "Not my story to tell."

He blew out a breath and began to explain. "I found her on my doorstep last night with a note saying she's mine."

"Jesus, Austin, ever hear of wrapping it up?" Damon asked from his seat on the couch.

He shot his brother a dirty look. "I did. But you know as well as I do, shit happens." He met his mother's gaze. "That's all I know right now. I called Ray Benson, my lawyer. He's going to arrange for a paternity test. I'll also turn the tapes from my house cameras over to a PI Ray uses, after I take a look and see if I recognize whoever left her."

"Jenny," his mother said. "Whoever left Jenny on your doorstep. She's a baby with a name." She continued to run her hand over the infant's back, and Jenny had her head resting on his mother's chest.

Even he wasn't immune to the sight of the sweet little thing in his mom's arms. But she was quiet for his mother. For Quinn. For him she shrieked like he was hurting her somehow.

"I know, Mom."

"But you haven't looked at her or asked to hold her since you walked in."

He hated the disappointment in her voice and expression. For his whole life, he'd strived to make his parents proud, but especially his mother. He cringed at the way she was looking at him now.

But it wasn't like he wasn't doing things for the baby. "I just spent the last two hours loading up my credit card with things for her. For Jenny. I don't know if she's mine and I'm trying to adjust."

"I don't care if she's yours or not. She needs love and affection. Attention, and it's not Quinn's responsibility."

"I didn't mind helping out, Mrs. Prescott," Quinn said quietly.

With the sound of her voice came the reminder that she was witnessing what felt like his shame. That he'd probably been responsible for creating a baby he hadn't known about. That his mother thought he was dropping the ball now.

"Call me Christine and I know you don't mind. I just want my son to understand this baby is his responsibility ... at least until we know whose baby she is. Although looking at these familiar blue eyes, I have a pretty good idea."

Austin reeled at the fact that his mother was con-
firming what his gut already knew. He leaned against
the nearest wall, totally floored. It was one thing to
suspect Jenny was his child, another to have the
closest person to him validate it.

"Mom, I need help," Austin said in a low voice. "I
need you."

His mother patted his face. "Honey, this is where a
man shows his true colors. I get that you need help,
but I have a cruise for my high school reunion that I
organized and I'm leaving in the morning. I can't not
show up. I'm the one in charge. I'm sorry. I'll be here
for you when I get back on Friday. I promise."

Shit. He'd totally forgotten her trip. "It's okay. I'll
figure something out."

Bri rose to her feet. "I'll stop by when I can but I
have that trip to LA with Manuel Rodriguez. It's his
first major sponsor photo shoot and I promised I'd be
there. What about a nanny?" she asked.

"I'll look into hiring someone, but it's going to
take time to vet people. I can't just trust anyone." He
knew he couldn't ask his brothers. They both had
team responsibilities, and if the idea of taking care of
an infant scared him, he doubted his bachelor brothers
with full-time careers were any more capable of
handling the baby.

No more than Austin himself. He had a business

to run, and though he could take time off if he needed to, the fact was, he didn't know how to deal with Jenny on his own. He was at a total loss and didn't know who to turn to or what to do.

"I'll do it. I'll move in and help," Quinn said, striding over to his mother and sliding a protective hand over little Jenny's head.

Everyone's eyes whipped toward her in shock but none more than Austin's.

Chapter Four

Q uinn didn't know what had possessed her to volunteer to move in with Austin and the baby. What in the ever-loving hell had she been thinking? One minute his family was giving valid reasons why they couldn't be there for him on such short notice, and the next her own voice rang out loud and clear.

Everyone in the room turned to face her and she felt a flush rush to her cheeks. "I can do it. Between Austin and me, we'll handle work and the baby."

She didn't mention she had enough experience with infants and children to juggle like the most capable nanny. She was the only person they had available, and they'd accept her help without her explaining her life story.

"Oh my God, Quinn, thank you." Austin stepped toward her and pulled her into an unexpected hug.

The scent of his cologne wrapped around her, sexy and sensual, and despite the fact that his family surrounded them and the gesture was due to gratitude, her body reacted immediately, memories of early this morning coming back to her in vivid detail. His demanding kiss, those forceful lips, the feel of his body grinding against her until she came.

A full-on rush of arousal hit her hard. Her nipples puckered under the borrowed tee shirt she still wore, and her panties grew damp. All because he held her against his rock-hard body. She wanted to rest her face in the crook of his neck and smell his skin.

Instead she stepped out of his embrace, sure her feelings were stamped all over her face, so she reached for Jenny and took the baby, hoping to hide her emotions behind the infant.

Then she made the mistake of peeking over Jenny's head and caught Austin's mother's knowing gaze. A pleased smile pulled at the other woman's lips, and Quinn knew she wasn't fooling anyone.

Including herself.

*   *   *

I'll do it. I'll move in and help.

As Austin and his brothers unloaded the truck, Quinn's words reverberated in Austin's head. Given how reticent she'd been about helping him in the first place, and the distance she'd placed between them since all but running from his bed this morning, he couldn't believe she'd offered to save his sorry ass.

He owed her a hell of a lot more than a raise. And that hug? He'd been so damned grateful, but the minute he'd pulled her into his arms, he'd felt much more. Dressed in his clothes, a turn-on in and of itself, she'd been so warm and soft, and when he'd breathed in, she'd smelled so good. His cock grew hard and his body craved hers.

But he knew how much he needed her help, so he needed to keep his hands—and his cock—to himself from now on. He didn't know how his life had gotten so fucked up in such a short amount of time, but he believed in coping with the hand he was dealt. So along with his brothers, they brought the baby items into the house from the truck.

While Bri, Quinn, and his mom unpacked, Austin headed downstairs to the basement. His brothers tagged along behind him to the walk-in closet where the camera recorder and screens were located.

"Do you have any idea who the mother of the baby is?" Damon asked as they entered the room. "Assuming she's yours, I mean."

Austin glanced at his youngest sibling, who still lived in the deluded world young athletes inhabited that nothing bad could touch them. "I have my suspicions, but I hope you take this as a lesson in being careful."

"Apparently condoms didn't work for you. Are you suggesting I become celibate?" Damon asked, chuckling at what he thought was his brilliant joke.

Jaxon smacked his brother in the head. "He's looking out for you, asshole."

In the middle of his career and still in his young, carefree bachelor days, when everything looked bright and new, Damon believed his own hype. He probably needed his ego checked, but that ego was what made him such a solid player. He'd learn over time that life wasn't all fun and games.

Austin began to fiddle with the equipment and rewound the tape to the time he'd been busy at the bar. He hoped like hell Jenny hadn't been left outside and alone for too long. The screen gave him multiple views of various angles of the house and driveway where he had cameras located or pitched, and he studied each.

Fast-forwarding, they watched as time passed, his brothers silent as they stared at the screen from behind him.

"There!" Jaxon pointed over Austin's shoulder. "Stop it now."

"I see." Austin pushed the pause button followed by rewind and then play.

At nine p.m., an hour before he'd gotten home, a gray-hooded figure held the carrier in one hand and the bag on her shoulder as she took the few steps up the porch. Austin assumed the person was a woman based on the slight build, but with her head and hair covered, there was no way to see a face.

After placing the baby on the ground along with the bag, she took the steps down and turned, staring at the infant for a minute before rushing away and out of camera range.

"Shit. We got nothing," Jaxon muttered.

"I honestly didn't think we would." But Austin pulled out a thumb drive he'd purchased at Target and duped the tape for his attorney and the PI on his payroll. "But I'll let the professionals go over it in case I missed something." He turned to his brothers. "Want to go upstairs and help set up my house for a baby?"

"This is surreal," Damon said. "But yeah, of course I'll help."

Austin laughed but he was still an anxious mess, and once back in the kitchen, he took in the bottles on the counter, the packages of formula beside them, and the reality of his situation sank in even more.

"We set up the pack and play in your room," his mother said. "And Jenny fell asleep immediately once we put her in there in a snuggly."

"The what and what?" Jaxon asked, sounding as confused as Austin had been in the store when he'd been looking for all the baby paraphernalia.

"The pack and play is a portable crib. Until we know for sure that she's mine, I'll make do with that," Austin explained.

"And the snuggly is a zipper-like thing that bundles the baby and makes her feel cocooned and safe," his mom said. "But if she is yours, you're going to need to turn one of the bedrooms into her room. You'll have to buy a real crib and furniture, and … I'll go shopping with you for all the baby things you didn't buy this trip."

Her excitement seemed to build and Austin knew he had to cut it off quickly. "I've got it, Mom. I know. But let's not rush things."

The truth was, he needed the time between now and when he learned the results of the paternity test to come to terms with his new potential reality. Thank God Quinn had agreed to help him.

He glanced around the room, seeing his brothers and his mother. "Where's Quinn and Bri? Are they upstairs?" He hoped he didn't sound as panicked as he felt at not seeing Quinn. In just one night, he'd grown used to her soothing presence to help with the baby. Hell, he was getting used to seeing her in his home, period. Besides, she'd promised she'd stick around.

"Bri went home with her so she could pack up a suitcase. She couldn't exactly live in your sweats and the same pair of underwear for the next five days." His mom took the lined-up bottles and began to put powdered formula in each. "I'm going to make you premade bottles and refrigerate them. That way you'll just have to heat them in the bottle warmer over there." She pointed to one of the items she'd set up.

He strode over and hugged his mother tight. "Thank you."

"You're welcome. Taking care of that adorable baby isn't a hardship. I can't wait to come back home and spend time with her. But I'm glad Quinn volunteered to stay. She's a sweet woman." His mother met his gaze. "In fact, I'd go so far as to say she's a keeper."

"Mom, are you matchmaking?" Jaxon asked with a snicker.

"Shut up, asshole. Wait until it's your turn."

His mother frowned. "Language, Austin. And I'm just saying she's good with the baby. And I might have seen how you look at her," she added under her breath.

"Jesus. I'm leaving before she finds a woman to hook me up with," Damon said. "You need anything, call me, bro. Just not for babysitting."

"I'll go with you." Jaxon slapped Austin on the shoulder. "I'll call and check on you. Behave with your assistant. You need her help, so don't go trying to get into her pants."

"Boys! Behave." Christine shook her head. "Now go. I need to teach your brother how to make bottles."

Jaxon snorted. "Love you, Mom."

"Love you, Mom," Damon repeated but they both obviously meant it. Then they walked out, bickering as they went.

*   *   *

Austin's mother waited until Quinn returned before she left, promising to check in later. Quinn had gone upstairs to unpack her things, leaving Austin in the kitchen he no longer recognized. The counters were strewn with bottles and nipples, his once clean house now a cluttered mess.

"Jesus. How did this happen?" he asked out loud, talking to himself.

Light laughter sounded as Quinn joined him in the brightly lit room. "Do you really want an answer?"

Knowing the direction of her thoughts, he shook his head.

She'd changed into a pair of black leggings and an extra-long red tank top. He was used to seeing her dressed for work, and the sight of her wearing casual clothes that showed off her body, her full breasts and curvy hips, had him drooling. When it came to Quinn, it didn't take much for her to have an impact.

He leaned against the counter and forced himself to focus. "Thanks for the help with the shopping list. And for everything else." He didn't know what he'd do if she hadn't stepped up.

"You're welcome. I'm not heartless and I won't leave you stranded without help."

He gestured toward the table and chairs and they settled in across from each other. He glanced at the baby monitor, which showed a sleeping infant, but his insides were jumping and he was nervous, waiting for her to wake up screaming at any moment.

He glanced at his assistant, who, in the last twenty-four hours, had shocked him with her baby abilities. He'd called her because he couldn't think of anyone else to help him, but he hadn't really expected that she'd be a pro.

"So tell me. How do you know so much about babies?" he asked.

Quinn blinked, obviously surprised by the question.

He leaned his arms on the table and studied her. "I mean, you jumped into the deep end with me like a champ. You knew exactly how to make a bottle, change a diaper, and calm a crying baby. Not to mention that shopping list. So where did all this knowledge come from?"

She sighed. "My family. It's big like yours. Both my parents worked and I'm the oldest." She shrugged. "They needed someone to watch the younger ones. And when my aunt had babies, it was always *Quinn can watch the kids*. It's not that I minded so much as that it was just expected."

"So while I was busy being pushed harder and harder in football, you were playing nanny."

Her pretty green eyes opened wide. "Exactly! It got to the point where my parents thought I might as well become a full-time childcare giver. Nobody ever considered I might have other dreams for my life."

He'd known her for a little over a year, and he'd never doubted her ability to run his office and business. "You're damned good at your job, Quinn. And what you didn't know about sports when you signed on, you learned on your own. I've always seen your drive to succeed."

Her cheeks flushed at the intended compliment. "Then you saw something my parents didn't. Even my brother doesn't really understand me. I'm glad you do."

As she met his gaze, an appreciative smile tilted her lips. "Look, I don't mind helping you out for a while but I love my job. And I never wanted kids. Not after raising everyone else's. So after you hire a nanny, I'm back to being your office assistant. Agreed?"

He swallowed hard, not understanding why her words caused a heavy weight in his chest. "Of course we're agreed. Besides, for all I know, Jenny's mother is going to show up any day and demand her daughter back."

At that, Quinn frowned. "She doesn't deserve to get Jenny back. Not after abandoning her on your doorstep."

"On that we agree." He didn't know what he was going to do about Jenny, and any time he thought about it, panic set in. So he'd just take each step as it came. He'd have a paternity test done. He'd hire a nanny. He'd figure things out.

Quinn propped her chin in her hands. "While we're sharing personal information, I'm curious how you accepted the news that Paul Dare was your father so easily? I started working for you right after you found out but you all seemed to handle it well."

He rose and walked to the refrigerator and pulled out a can of soda. "Can I get you something?"

She shook her head. "No, thanks. I'm good."

He popped the top and took a long sip before meeting her gaze, taking the time to figure out how to explain his unusual family situation.

"You know how you said nobody asked you what you wanted to do in your family?" He walked back to the table and sat down once more. "Well, nobody asked me what my dreams were, either. My father, the one who raised us, was a hard-ass bastard, if you want to know the truth."

"How?" she asked softly.

"He wanted to live his lost dreams through us.

He'd always planned to play pro football but an injury derailed him. Then, as we know now, he couldn't have kids. Suffice to say, he was angry and bitter. But if he couldn't play, his boys damn well would." Jesse Prescott's no-choice attitude had pervaded the household.

"I guess that explains all the athletes in your family," Quinn mused.

Austin pulled another long sip of bubbly soda. "In part. The truth is, I always excelled at the sport and I wanted to play and make the pros. But Dad ... Jesse ... he worked us hard. He coached. And if I lost, I had to walk home from the game. At ten years old. Same for my brothers." The memory caused an old ache to open up inside him, and his muscles stiffened as the memories returned.

"That's awful." Quinn's soft hand covered his.

He shrugged. "I had it easier than Jaxon, who preferred baseball to football. That pissed Dad off. And Damon was good, but football didn't come as naturally to him as it did to me. So he had it hard, too. And Braden? The one with the brains and no desire to be a jock?" Austin shook his head, not wanting to subject her to the yelling that used to go on in the house. All the while his mother would try and play mediator.

"But back to your question, Paul was our pseudo-uncle. The voice of reason to Jesse's irrational behavior. He was always there for all of us. So finding out that Paul was our biological father was almost a relief."

Quinn squeezed his hand tighter. "Yeah, I get it now. Becoming a Dare was actually a good thing."

He grinned. "The fact that being a Dare came with a shit ton of cousins? That was unexpected and it's been surreal getting to know them a little at a time." He laughed as he said, "There are a lot of Dares."

She chuckled. "I know a little something about big families."

"We do have that in common." Before he could say more, a loud wail pierced his ears, sounding like it came from directly across the room. He turned and caught sight of the baby monitor that showed Jenny winding up as she let out another ear-splitting cry.

"I'll get her. Can you heat a bottle?" Quinn asked.

And just like that, their warm bonding moment was over.

*   *   *

Quinn and Austin passed the weekend taking care of the baby, with her teaching Austin the minute details of infant care, including diaper changing, because Quinn refused to pull all the heavy duty. He was by no means a pro but he was definitely getting the hang of things. But after dinner, and giving Jenny a bath, which had been an experience in and of itself because

Austin hadn't been prepared for babies to be so slippery, they'd put her to bed.

And Quinn rushed to her own room, admitting she was a coward. Their conversation this afternoon had shown her Austin was a real man with past pain just like she had. But if they were going to take care of Jenny together, Quinn needed to be smart. The last thing she ought to do was fall for her boss. One day she hoped to find a real love, and Austin didn't do long-term or serious relationships. And now he potentially had a practically newborn baby while Quinn was finished raising other people's kids.

Finally, Monday arrived and they returned to work. Quinn stood at her desk in the office, Jenny strapped to her chest in a Baby Bjorn. Jenny wouldn't settle down in the car seat carrier and she clearly needed snuggles and body contact. If not for the fact that Austin had a meeting with Ian Dare, a team owner and his cousin on Paul Dare's side, she'd have strapped the baby to Austin and enjoyed watching him squirm.

It was actually endearing, the way he was trying to get comfortable with Jenny. Last night, while Quinn had showered, he'd laid the baby on his bed and talked to her in a gallant effort to keep Jenny from becoming hysterical. Holding her hadn't worked. Austin was still too tense, hence Quinn's determination to strap him to the baby for some bonding time soon.

But it never failed, just as Austin lifted the baby against him, Jenny's little lips would pucker and she'd pull in short, panicked breaths, obviously not knowing what to make of the new man in her life. So he'd placed her down on his mattress and made the cutest baby noises and faces at her.

If Austin realized Quinn had snuck to the doorway to watch, he'd have been mortified. As for her, all the viewing had done was serve to ramp up her desire for the man. Hot, sexy, and he put his all into everything he did, including attempting to be a dad to a baby he didn't know for sure was his.

Doing her normal routine, she was filing papers, Jenny dozing against her. Most of their system was computerized, but there were recent things they wanted to get their hands on quickly so they printed and she organized.

"Excuse me. Quinn?" a masculine voice said.

She turned to see Ian Dare standing at her desk. As his football team was located in Miami, Ian had been a frequent visitor to Dare Nation since Quinn began working there. More often since he and Austin had been pronounced family.

"Hello, Mr. Dare."

"I told you to call me Ian." He looked at her and his eyes opened wide. "What the hell are you doing with a baby?" Ian Dare was known for being blunt, often to a fault, but he had been around her often enough to know that she hadn't been pregnant and the baby wasn't hers.

"Umm..." She and Austin hadn't discussed how she should handle questions. Ian was his first appointment of the day, and Quinn had a feeling a part of him was still in denial.

On the way to work, she'd offered to start looking into nanny agencies and set up appointments with potential candidates and he'd agreed. So she'd begun researching agencies and would discuss possibilities with him tonight, but for now...

"She's mine. Maybe." Austin stepped out of his office and strode over to Ian. "Good to see you," he said, extending his hand.

Ian shook it, but his expression was still one of utter shock. "I assume you'll explain."

Austin nodded. "How's Jenny doing?" His gaze settled on Quinn, warming her from the inside out.

"She's good." Quinn smiled and his stare lowered to her lips.

She swallowed hard and forced herself to focus on both men instead of being obvious in her desire for Austin.

Now that she knew the men were cousins, the similarities were unmistakable. The dark hair, same indigo eyes. Ian was more staid and uptight than Austin, his hair well cut while Austin's was longer, sexier. While Ian wore a suit and tie, Austin presented a more relaxed but no less potent version of utter masculinity in a pair of well-tailored black slacks and a light blue button-down shirt, sleeves folded up neatly. And where Ian had shaved this morning, Austin had a sexy scruff she often wondered about. How would that light beard feel rubbing against her thighs as he went down on her?

She cleared her throat. "Can I get either of you water, coffee, or anything?" Her gaze encompassed both men, and she hoped the warmth she felt on her cheeks wasn't obvious.

"No, thank you," Ian said.

"I'm good." Austin smiled at her, and the sinful grin didn't help alleviate the ache her dirty thoughts had caused. "Quinn, hold my calls please," he said, gesturing for Ian to head into his office.

Knowing he wanted to discuss his brother's final year under contract with Ian, she nodded. "Will do."

Ian headed into the office, and instead of following him, Austin walked over to her, sidling up close. His warm scented cologne sent her senses into overdrive. "How are you really doing?" he asked her.

She swallowed hard. "I'm okay. She's fast asleep and a good baby."

He leaned down and kissed the top of Jenny's

head, his hair brushing against Quinn's cheek, causing a further spike of arousal she didn't need.

That was the sweetest thing she'd ever seen and definitely worked on softening her heart toward this always enigmatic man. Danger surrounded her at every turn, and her emotions and heart were in the most jeopardy.

*   *   *

Whenever Austin found himself in the presence of one of the Dares, they always made him feel welcome. Like family. Ian wasn't an exception. In fact, he'd been the first to reach out after Paul broke the news about being their biological father. And despite their new familial status, Austin and Ian still managed to negotiate like business owners, without personal feelings getting involved.

Austin lowered himself into the chair behind his desk and met Ian's gaze, noting the questions clearly etched on his cousin's face.

"Well? Are you going to explain the infant dangling from your assistant's chest?" Ian asked in the wake of the silence surrounding them.

"I found her on my doorstep Friday night." Austin shifted in his seat. This was the first time other than his immediate family that he'd had to explain Jenny's presence. It wouldn't be the last, either.

"No shit?" Ian asked.

"Nope."

"And you *think* she's yours?" Ian asked.

Scrubbing a hand over his face, Austin groaned. "The note left with her says she's mine. Based on how old we think she is, the timing seems to work, but of course I'm having a DNA test run. My lawyer said he'd have someone stop by tomorrow to swab us and handle getting the results." He hadn't let himself deal with what he'd do in either case.

"And how's it going with the baby?" Ian astutely asked.

Austin frowned. "She takes one look at me and screams like I'm an ax murderer." But she really was adorable with those big blue eyes and chubby cheeks.

His cousin chuckled, leaning back in his chair. "Babies take getting used to. I should know. I've had three. Rainey is five going on eighteen, Jack is two, and baby Gracie is almost a year old," he said, his voice softening at the mention of his children. "But they're the best and you should enjoy it while she's young. Assuming she's yours."

Austin groaned. "I don't know how you do it. One is killing me. My kitchen's been taken over by bottles and my house by baby equipment, and she wakes me in the middle of the night screaming."

"So you have your executive assistant helping you

out?" Ian asked.

Austin nodded. "Quinn is the only one who can step in right now, and she's got the magic touch. The baby adores her."

"As do you?" Ian tapped his foot against the floor. His expression indicated he'd already drawn his own conclusion about Quinn and Austin.

And he'd be correct. But she'd put a solid wall between them when she'd admitted she didn't want kids while he had the feeling Jenny was, in fact, his.

His life had become fucking complicated, because ever since he'd felt Quinn beneath him, his cock grinding into her pussy, separated only by thin underwear, his desire for her had merely increased. In addition to how his heart sped up when watching her with Jenny? It wasn't like him. Nothing going on in his life right now was like him.

Ian studied him intently. "I saw how you looked at Quinn today. I've been there, and trust me, I suggest you lock that down before someone else shows up and steps in first." Ian probably wasn't joking, either.

Austin had heard about how Ian's wife, Riley, had been his half brother Alex's best friend. Ian had come between Riley and Alex, and though they'd never been a couple, from Ian's possessive tone, that hadn't mattered. According to Dare family lore, Ian had worked hard to win Riley, and once he had her, he kept her pregnant and happy.

The thought of another man making a play for Quinn didn't sit well with Austin, but he didn't have a say. Picking up a pen on his desk, he rolled it between his palms, thinking about the woman outside his office.

"She doesn't want kids," he admitted to Ian. "She's already all but raised her siblings and cousins. Which means whatever I might be feeling for her doesn't matter as long as Jenny is mine."

Ian studied him. "In my case, what Riley thought she didn't want and what she was afraid of were one and the same. Once I got her past her issues, she became mine."

Austin heard the man but he believed Quinn knew her own mind. And she'd said she didn't want children. Austin believed her.

"What if the baby isn't yours? I happened to turn and notice that little kiss you gave her. Looks to me like you're already falling for the baby, too," Ian said with certainty.

His words hit home, but unsure how to respond, Austin remained silent.

Ian cocked his head to one side. "Look, I'm giving you things to think about. I just want you to be happy. Like I want for everyone in my family. Now let's talk business."

Jesus, the man could cause whiplash, Austin thought and refocused himself on his clients and what was in their best interest. "Fine. Damon's contract is up at the end of the season. He'll be a free agent. I've had other teams sniffing around. Is there a reason I should take them seriously?" His brother wanted to remain in Miami, but no need to tell Ian that and tip his hand.

Ian folded his arms across his chest, his face impassive, giving nothing away, either. "If he plays the same way this year as last, we'll talk."

"You know he will."

He shrugged as if to say, *we'll see.*

They discussed a few other mutual clients and Ian rose to his feet. "We should get together. Riley loves babies and maybe you'll pick up some tips." Ian grinned. "I'll text you some items that might save your life."

"I'd appreciate that. As for getting together, give me a week or so to settle in with Jenny and to make sure she's really mine." If she was, his entire life would remain as it was now, upside down and brand-new. If she wasn't his, what was he going to do? Give her up to social services and some unknown family?

He'd only had Jenny in his home for a weekend, but she was a helpless infant and she needed loving care. Not a family who took her in for cash or had other kids and couldn't give her the love and time she deserved.

Both thoughts churned his already upset stomach.

Chapter Five

Austin had convinced Quinn to let him drive them to and from work since they were coming and going from the same place anyway. She figured people in the office would learn she was helping him out with the baby, so she didn't have to hide them arriving together.

When they returned home at the end of the day, he parked and she noticed a huge box sitting on the front step. "What is that?" she asked.

"A baby swing. Amazon had same-day delivery." He opened the truck door and hopped out, leaving her speechless.

She let herself out and met him by the back door on the baby's side. He'd already begun unbuckling the car seat and lifting Jenny into his arms.

Stunned, she followed him up the steps and unlocked the front door.

"Can you hold her so I can get the box inside?" he asked.

"Sure." Her head was spinning, shocked he hadn't expected her to take Jenny out of the seat. "You're suddenly comfortable with her?"

He grunted in response, then said, "Not really. But I had an interesting conversation with Ian." Austin dragged the box into the house.

She followed him and he shut the door, locking it behind him.

"Ian has three kids, and for some reason it got me thinking about what Jenny needs." He rested a hand on the top of the box. "She needs *me*. Right now I'm all she has." He met her gaze. "*We're* all she has."

"For now," she felt compelled to remind him. She wasn't his or Jenny's answer to life.

He frowned and continued. "Anyway, Ian sent me a list of some items that he said would give us a break from holding her constantly. The swing being one of them."

Quinn forced a grin. "If I'm the baby whisperer, Ian must be the Austin whisperer."

He rolled his eyes. "If you don't mind feeding her, I'll get this set up. Oh, and do you want to order dinner?"

She nodded, and later, they shared Chinese food out of cartons. Sitting side by side on the couch in the family room, they watched Jenny swing back and forth. Freshly bathed, fed, and changed, she was quiet and happy in her new piece of equipment, her little feet kicking, while Austin was extremely proud of himself for buying and setting up the swing.

He was already something to see as a man. Watching him come into his own as a dad was sexy in a whole different way. She didn't *want* to see Austin as the whole package, and she reminded herself that not only did he not want a long-term relationship, *she* preferred to be alone. Or with a man who didn't come with a built-in family. Hadn't she broken up with Daniel for the very reason that she didn't want children? And that hadn't changed.

She looked from the swinging baby to the man beside her.

"So tell me, really, are you okay with your new reality?" she asked him. "Or are you just making the best of it?"

He paused with the fork halfway to his mouth and lowered it to the table. "Frankly, I'm scared to death."

She blinked in surprise because he'd suddenly seemed so capable and calm.

"There's a baby in that swing that a note says is mine," he went on. "A woman floating around out there who could show up at any minute and demand her back. A DNA test to be taken that could change my entire life, and these last three days have given me a glimpse as to just how drastically. So no. I'm really not okay. I'm just doing what I have to do for that helpless little baby."

He expelled a long breath, and she finally realized just how much this situation was impacting him.

"Hey." She put her own fork down. "I know this is rough. I'm not going to bail on you until you get yourself settled one way or another. And your mother will be home before you know it so she can pitch in. You aren't alone."

His gaze warmed at her words but he looked upset. "Except I am alone. *You* said you don't want kids? Hell, *I* never gave them a thought. And what's worse is that I was careful. I know for sure I used a condom. So to say this is unexpected is an understatement." He ran a hand through his hair and messed up the long strands.

She blew out a breath. "I—"

"Do you know what's worse?" He interrupted her and she waved a hand for him to continue.

Obviously he had things he needed to get off his chest.

"What the fuck do I know about being a father?" He stabbed himself in the chest with his finger. "Jesse Prescott taught me lessons in berating a kid to get the best out of him. How's that for a good role model?"

"Oh, Austin." She leaned in close and wrapped her arm around his shoulders. "You're not Jesse. You're a good man. You've put your life on hold to take care of a little girl you aren't even certain is yours. Forgetting

the fact that you spent a small fortune in baby sup-
plies, you've learned how to change a diaper and give a
bottle when you could have turned her over to the
police, who would have given her to CPS."

He shook his head. "Those are basics. Anyone can
do that."

"But not just anyone would. Just like being a kidney donor for Paul. You stepped up." She stroked a
hand down his cheek, feeling the stubble beneath her
fingertips. "If you're her father, you're going to be a
good dad. I promise."

He managed a smile but she knew it was half-
hearted at best.

A muscle still worked in his jaw from the way he
obviously clenched his teeth. "Listen, I need some
time to think. I'm going to go out to the pool for a bit
and just chill. Can you handle her if she wakes up?"

She swallowed hard, hating that she'd upset him.
"Of course. And I'll clean up." She reached out to
touch him in reassurance, but he rose, turned, and
walked away.

*   *   *

Austin stood facing the Olympic-sized pool that had
been a selling point of the house. The ability to swim
laps in order to unwind was always something he
enjoyed. Tonight was a cool evening for August, and

he wasn't in the mood to go into the water. He'd just needed to be alone to think.

Ever since he'd accepted the reality of Jenny in his home, he'd been forcing thoughts of Jesse out of his mind. He'd even tried to be okay with the situation after Ian had left, but the more he attempted to be the upbeat, good father she needed, the more insidious thoughts of the dad who'd raised him intruded. And Quinn had called him on it.

Somehow she sensed all wasn't as it seemed and he'd dumped his fears on her. Not his greatest moment, he thought. Another thing Jesse had instilled in him. Never show weakness.

Except, when it came to the woman currently living in his house, he was beginning to feel his personal walls crumble. And if he wasn't careful, he was going to be left having to pick up the pieces when she was gone.

* * *

Sitting at her desk in the office the next morning, Quinn looked at the schedule for the day. She'd found a bonded nanny agency that agreed to send qualified candidates with vetted references over to Dare Nation for interviews. She'd explained the urgency of the situation, and she had five women coming to the office today.

Again, she worked with Jenny, alternating between the car seat carrier and the Baby Bjorn. If she wasn't such a sweet baby, this situation wouldn't have been palatable, but she was. So Quinn was able to handle it. And there was a small part of her that was falling for the adorable infant, which made her grateful Austin's mother would be home in a couple of days and relieve her of duty.

The first candidate arrived, a young woman with stars in her eyes, and when she caught sight of the athlete photographs on the walls in the office, those eyes lit up. Quinn disliked her immediately and was grateful when Austin cut the interview short after she was visibly sucking up to him and ignoring the baby.

Candidate number two was an older woman with strict ideas about babies, scheduling, letting them cry it out, and other old-school ideas that had Quinn cringing at the thought of subjecting Jenny to such a rigid woman.

"Thank you, we'll be in touch," Quinn had said, interrupting the woman mid-sentence.

Austin, she'd noted, hid a grin as Quinn had risen from her chair and escorted the other woman out, listening to her complain that Quinn hadn't let her finish discussing the Ferber method of teaching a baby to self-soothe. It hadn't helped that she'd gone into a lecture on the issues with the Baby Bjorn and spoiling an infant.

The day went on in similar fashion, with either Quinn or Austin finding reasons to dislike the candidates.

And when someone from the lab arrived to take a DNA swab from Austin and Jenny, Austin hovered over the baby and asked a ton of questions, making the entire process take longer than it should have for a mere mouth swab.

On top of that, his lawyer had no leads on the baby's mother. Austin had visibly tensed when he'd taken the call and hadn't been happy with no progress, and Quinn had had to remind him it had only been a few days.

Quinn was giving the baby a bottle when Paul Dare walked up to her desk.

"Hi, Quinn." The handsome man treated her to a warm smile. He had a full head of dark hair, tanned skin, and a healthy pallor, thanks to Austin.

"Hi, Mr. Dare."

He frowned. "Paul, please. I've told you that."

She nodded. "I'm sorry. Habit." Her parents had instilled the Mr. and Mrs. thing and it had stuck.

He glanced at the baby in her arms. "Quite the change around here, yes?" The good-looking older man met her gaze and grinned.

She nodded.

"And no news from the child's mother?" Paul asked.

"If you mean has she shown up or been found, that's a big *no*." She glanced down at Jenny, who stared at her with eyes very similar to the man standing in front of Quinn.

She had a feeling Austin had every right to be concerned that the baby was his. And just as much right to worry if she wasn't, because who in the world would take care of her then? Quinn's stomach churned at the uncomfortable thought.

"Is he in? Or is he with a client?" Paul tipped his head toward the closed door.

"He's in. I'll let him know you're here."

"I'll just surprise him. You have your hands full," he said before she could get a handle on juggling the baby, the bottle, and the phone.

"I appreciate it." She was glad Paul was here to talk to Austin, because she had a feeling he needed his uncle's support more than he realized.

* * *

"Austin."

At the sound of his uncle's voice, Austin turned away from the window overlooking the city of Miami. "Hi. I didn't hear you come in."

"You're preoccupied. Understandably so." Paul

strode over and put an arm around his shoulders. "It's not every day a man finds out he's a father and is handed his baby in one day."

Austin let out a rough laugh. "I guess that sums it up. If she's mine." He was getting tired of that refrain, but the lab tech told him that his law firm had paid for rushed results, so the best he could hope for was three to five working days.

He stepped away from his uncle and walked over to the makeshift bar he kept in his office. "Can I make you a drink? Club soda and a splash of cranberry juice?"

Since Paul's transplant, he'd sworn off alcohol, determined to make his single kidney last.

"Sounds good."

Austin nodded. "I'll have one, too. I could use the hard stuff today." He chuckled at his own joke and poured two virgin drinks, handing one to his uncle.

"Let's sit," Paul said, choosing a club chair in a corner where Austin had a comfortable, casual den-like area set up in his overly large office.

Austin lowered himself into the matching chair to Paul's and crossed one leg over his knee. "So. To what do I owe this visit? Want to discuss Damon's upcoming year? Another client contract?"

"No. What I want is to get you to open up and relieve yourself of the panic I know must be riding you.

So tell me what's on your mind? What's wrong besides the obvious?"

Taking a sip of his drink, Paul studied him in silence. The man had a knack for getting others to talk because he had the ability to remain quiet down to an art form.

Austin ran a hand over his face and groaned. "What isn't wrong?" Without drinking any, he put his glass onto a coaster. "Let's see. There's a woman floating around out there who is Jenny's mother. Let's assume for the moment the baby is mine. That means I'm stuck with this crazy person for the rest of my life. Joint custody or a custody fight. Something is brewing. There's no way she just dropped the baby off and is going to disappear." The longer he chewed on the situation, the more he was certain.

Jenny's mother wanted something. Why else leave her baby on his doorstep? At the thought, what was becoming a familiar pain lodged in his chest. He didn't know if the discomfort was because of the disruption Jenny being his baby would cause ... or the baby's mother's unknown intentions. He rubbed on his sternum in a futile attempt to ease it.

Paul leaned in close. "I can understand you find that upsetting, but until you have the DNA test back so you can formalize your rights to the baby, there's nothing you can do."

He nodded. "I know that."

"Your mother will be back from her cruise at the end of the week. You and Quinn will have backup." He took another sip. "A little less cranberry next time," he said with a laugh.

Austin grinned. "Good to know my bartending skills aren't up to par." He hesitated then said, "What if she's mine? What do I know about being a father? Or being a single parent? Because I don't want someone who can abandon their child anywhere near my kid." His certainty on that was clear.

Paul's expression gentled. "You know kindness and empathy. And you know what not to do." Paul met his gaze, so much unsaid yet understood between them.

"That's what Quinn said," Austin admitted. He wasn't a man used to unburdening himself, but that's what seemed to be happening and often lately.

"She's a smart woman. And she also has a big heart," Paul said.

Austin grinned at that. "Yeah, she does."

"The question is, does she have yours?"

He shook his head. "What is it with people asking me how I feel about my assistant?"

Paul lifted an eyebrow. "So I'm not the only one who noticed how your eyes follow her wherever she goes."

Austin ignored the words, his fingers toying with the material on his slacks.

"You and Ian are seeing things," he said at last. As was his mother, but he wasn't about to make things worse for himself by admitting even the astute Christine had nailed his feelings for a woman he couldn't have.

Paul's concerned gaze rested on his. "Son, life is short. I, of all people, know that. I came close to not getting that kidney because I didn't want to risk the secret I'd agreed to hold years ago. It was your mother who convinced me to talk to all of you."

Austin's heart skipped a beat at the thought of losing a man who'd treated him better than his own father had. "I realize that."

"Then you should go after what you want. Just because you hadn't planned on a family doesn't mean you shouldn't have one. Can't have one. Or don't deserve one."

His uncle's words settled him somewhat. "I hear you. It's just ... there are a lot of pieces that have to fall into place and I've barely adjusted to the possibility of any of them. But I appreciate your wisdom and I'll keep it in mind."

"Good." Paul rose and placed a hand briefly on Austin's shoulder. Then, picking up his drink, he walked to the bar and poured it into the sink, causing

Austin to laugh.

"Point taken. Less cranberry juice."

Paul grinned. "And now I'm going for lunch with Ron." He started for the door and turned. "I love you, Austin."

Austin swallowed hard. "Love you, too."

He stood and walked his uncle to the door, opening it in time to see and hear Quinn pat Jenny on her back and the infant let out a large, loud burp.

He laughed, causing Quinn to look his way. "Give her to me. I'll put her down," he said, picking the little girl off Quinn's shoulder and gently placing her into the carrier.

She was already asleep, full and completely satisfied, he thought, as he stood up.

Paul looked from Austin to Quinn and back again. "You two make a good team."

She blushed and Austin wanted to strangle his uncle.

"I love my job here. But I could really use a breather, so if you'll watch Jenny, I'm going to pick something up for lunch." In a frenzy, Quinn gathered her purse and some other items. His uncle's words and innuendo had obviously rattled her.

"Sure thing," he said, understanding she needed time to herself. She'd been at his beck and call since Friday night.

He waited until Quinn had walked out of hearing range before turning to his uncle. "Does that look like a woman who's ready for a relationship, let alone a built-in family?"

Without waiting for an answer, he picked up the carrier handle and walked into his office, closing the door behind him.

*   *   *

By the time they were ready to leave work, Quinn was exhausted, and when they arrived at the house, she was only too happy to let Austin give Jenny a bottle. She had other things to handle around the house. But when she walked into Jenny's room with the intention of gathering her laundry, she discovered his house-keeper had been there and washed the baby's dirty clothes, sheets, and blankets.

And in her bedroom, the laundry basket was empty as well. Although she was grateful, she didn't want to make extra work for anyone while she was here. Still, it meant she had some time to herself tonight, and my God, did she need it. Austin could spend time with Jenny.

She needed a distraction and decided to go for a swim and eat something for dinner afterwards. Having seen the pool when she was here once before, she'd tossed her bathing suit in along with her clothes on a whim, and now she was glad that she had.

After grabbing a towel from her bathroom, she headed down to the pool, but not wanting to talk, she bypassed the kitchen and family room where Austin might be and headed out to the backyard through a side door.

She placed her towel on a chair and dove into the deep end. The perfect-temperature water washed over her and she broke the surface, immediately starting laps. With each stroke, she let her mind wander to the sudden changes in her life.

As cute as the baby was, Quinn wasn't used to being responsible for anyone but herself. It had been a long time since she'd had childcare duties, and she'd forgotten how tiring a day could be. And though she was getting her work done in the office, she couldn't deny she missed her normal routine. But then Jenny would open those blue eyes and stare her down, and Quinn would melt like chocolate in the summertime, pick her up, and spend time cooing at her like a nut.

She was such a sucker for babies, which surprised her considering how adamant she was about not wanting kids of her own. And then there was Austin.

Last week, he'd been her boss. A man she'd kissed once and put it out of her mind. Or at least, she'd tried to forget that sensual meeting of their lips and his deeply masculine taste.

There had been so many reasons she couldn't get involved with him then, from not risking her job to not wanting to get involved with a man who didn't do relationships. In the year she'd been working for him, she'd never seen him with any one woman twice. Same for his past, if the internet was to be believed. And the fact was, Quinn did want a man in her life. A partner who understood her needs, her drive, and her desire to work.

Now suddenly she was living with her boss and his possible baby, she'd come apart in his arms, she was caring for said infant, and her life had been turned upside down. She consoled herself with the fact that by Friday his mother would return, Quinn could go home, and everything would return to normal.

But for some reason, even knowing that, the pit in her stomach remained, anxiety a sudden part of her she didn't understand.

*　　*　　*

Austin heard a door slam shut, and since he hadn't seen Quinn walk by, he assumed she'd gone out back to the pool. If anyone had been stressed and needed a break, it'd been Quinn and for that he felt bad.

He walked to the window in his bedroom that overlooked the yard and saw her on the pool deck wearing a formfitting racing suit that showed off that gorgeous body he'd only had glimpses of in a short camisole. His dick immediately responded, and when she dove into the water, all slick grace, he groaned, wanting nothing more than to be there with her.

She was a special woman. From the moment he'd called her in a panic, she'd been there for him. She'd stepped up and taken care of Jenny like she was a born mother, despite the fact that she'd since admitted she didn't want children. But with every minute that passed, he came to appreciate her more and more. He watched her as she swam to the end of the pool, drew a breath, turned, and headed toward the front end.

His thoughts went to their tag-teaming of nannies today. He'd rejected candidates because none were good enough for Jenny. Quinn had done the same, as if she had a say in the decision. As far as Austin was concerned, she did. In his mind, no one else could supply the baby with the love, attention, and complete understanding that Quinn seemed to give her. Though it had only been a couple of days, he couldn't imagine his life without her in it.

Ian was right.

His uncle had a valid point.

Austin desired his assistant.

He scrubbed a hand over his face, wondering what to do, and then he decided. Fuck it. He was going down to join her.

He shucked his shirt and swapped his pants for a pair of swim trunks, grabbed the baby monitor, and headed downstairs.

He strode through the house and opened the sliding glass doors leading outside, stepping into the hot, humid air. Quinn was still swimming laps, gliding through the water with fluid movements. He placed the monitor on a small table and turned up the volume so he'd hear the baby if she woke up.

Then he walked into the shallow end, taking the two steps down to the pool, and waited until Quinn swam toward him, stopping when she reached him. She stood, brushing the water off her face and out of her eyes. Her dark hair hung to her shoulders. Her breasts were full in the suit, her nipples hardened into tight peaks. His own body responded, and if she looked, there was no way she'd miss his erection.

But those her green eyes narrowed on his. "What brings you out here?"

"The pool looked inviting." And so had she.

"I thought so, too. I needed to get rid of my frustrations. Today drove me insane. I can't believe we couldn't find a nanny," she said.

"Are there more people coming tomorrow?"

She shook her head. "Since we need someone so quickly, they sent out their best people today. The woman who runs the agency is going to put out the word she's looking for the right type of nanny. But I had an idea. It came to me just now while I was swimming."

"I'm all ears." He walked to the side of the pool and sat on the edge.

She joined him, hopping up next to him. "Remember I told you I have a huge family? Well, those cousins I used to babysit for are grown up now. I have one who is going to college in September, but she didn't find a job for the summer. I could see if she wants to babysit while we're at work. It wouldn't cover the nights, but at least Jenny would have someone capable at home during the day."

"Really? That would be amazing." His work life could return to some semblance of normalcy, and Quinn wouldn't have to juggle Jenny and her normal daily business.

"*If* she wants to do it. The choice has to be hers," Quinn said, her tone adamant.

"Because nobody gave you the choice?" he guessed.

She raised her eyebrows, obviously surprised. "You remember I said that?"

He nodded. "Of course I do. And it didn't escape my notice that I pretty much did the same thing to you when I called and all but demanded your help."

Her lips lifted in a smile. "At least you recognize it.

That puts you way beyond my family."

He raised a hand, ran a finger down her cheek, enjoying the silky-smooth feel of her skin. "I try to be self-aware. You should know, the fact that I asked you to help me with Jenny? It's because I trust you."

She shivered at his touch, and her nipples hardened even more beneath the thin bathing suit. His mouth watered with the desire to pull down the stretch material, view her breasts for the first time, and pull one rigid nipple into his mouth.

"I also want you," he said in a thick voice.

Her frown took him off guard. "Do you? Or do you want the built-in nanny I provide? One you *trust*," she said, throwing his words back at him.

"That's not fair." She'd twisted his words to mean something different than he'd intended. He dropped his hand from her face, letting it rest on the strap of her bathing suit, his fingers running beneath the stretch material.

"No? Don't you realize what getting involved with me looks like? It looks like we're together, and God knows you're not the relationship type."

He narrowed his gaze at her words. He couldn't deny they were true. Well, they *had* been true at one time. "Maybe I wasn't the relationship type. Doesn't mean I can't change for the right woman."

Her eyes opened wide. "Come on, Austin. I already told you I don't want kids, so you can't possibly think I'm that right woman for you. Besides, I've seen your type. And she's not the executive assistant with a brain. She's the woman who runs at the first sign of trouble. Or an infant, as the case may be."

He winced. "Touché. But that doesn't mean I don't desire you. And I'm not asking for a future you don't want. I'm asking for tonight."

She swallowed hard and he knew he was getting to her.

"Can you deny the attraction between us?" He continued to rub his finger along her shoulder, sliding up to her collarbone, and watched her tremble beneath his touch. "I want you, Quinn. *You.* Not what you can do for me." And if this was all he could have with her, he'd take it.

Her mouth parted slightly as she obviously considered his words.

He slid his hand around her neck and pulled her toward him. "Let me show you how good we can be together."

Without waiting, he sealed his lips over hers and made his point the only way he knew how. By devouring her in the most intimate way.

Chapter Six

Quinn didn't want to push Austin away. She wanted him as much as he desired her, and she'd be foolish not to give in.

After all, he understood what she did and didn't want out of her future. He respected her. One night was just what she needed to get Austin Prescott out of her system.

With that thought, she parted her lips and let his tongue tangle with hers. What started as a teasing kiss quickly turned hot. He nipped at her bottom lip, readjusted their mouths, and thrust his tongue deeper into her waiting mouth.

She lifted her hands, threaded her fingers in the longer strands of his hair. He did the same. He tilted her head so he could kiss her harder, and she leaned into him, deliberately brushing her breasts against his chest.

He groaned and pulled back. "Inside now. I can't do what I want to you with concrete surrounding us."

She blinked, dazed by the kiss, her sex wet and not just from the pool. Desire pulsed inside her, and somehow she managed a nod. He rose and held out a hand, helping her to her feet. She grabbed a towel and wrapped it around herself, drying off, just as he snagged the monitor and they headed inside.

They entered his bedroom and he put the monitor on the table. Then he turned to her and yanked the towel off her and tossed it onto the floor.

"Undress," he said in a gruff voice. "I'd do it but I have a feeling that bathing suit is just too tight for me to work off of you myself."

She nodded. "It is." And while she tugged the straps off first one shoulder, then the other, he pulled his own bathing suit down and kicked it aside.

She took one look at his thick, hard cock and let out a low moan.

"I'm glad you like what you see, but you're still dressed." A sexy smile curved his lips.

Blushing, she pulled her bathing suit down, revealing her breasts to the cool air conditioning and his heated gaze. Her nipples puckered tighter, almost to the point of pain.

"More," he said in a strangled tone.

She hooked her fingers into the sides and wriggled the suit over her hips, bending to take it down her legs, and picked it up off the floor and placed the damp suit on the dresser.

His approving stare ate her up, and she did her

best not to squirm beneath his appraisal.

"Jesus, you're beautiful." Reaching out, he cupped one breast in his hand, testing the weight, rubbing his thumb over the tight peak.

Desire shot straight to her sex, and she rubbed her thighs together at the same moment he dipped his head and pulled her nipple into his mouth. He grazed his teeth over her, licked and soothed the tiny bite, and suckled her nipple into his mouth. She grabbed on to his head, aware of his dark hair grazing her chest and the groan that came from deep inside his throat.

Without warning, he released her nipple with a pop, bent and lifted her into his arms. Next thing she knew, she was on the bed, and Austin crawled over her, his hard cock a hot rod against her belly. His mouth came down on hers for another hard kiss while he ground his erection against her pussy.

She writhed beneath him, enjoying the hot friction, but he didn't remain there long enough for her to come. He slid down her body and parted her legs, baring her completely.

Startled, she met his darkened gaze.

"I'm dying to know what you taste like." His voice sounded gruff and sexy.

Before she could process the words, he dipped his head and did just that, his tongue taking a long lap over her pussy. Her hips bucked, but he placed a hand

over her belly, holding her in place, and then he
devoured her. She didn't know a man's tongue could
be that talented, but her hips rocked, her back arched,
and soon she was grinding herself against his mouth.
He flicked her clit back and forth until she couldn't
take another second, and then she was flying, coming
hard and crying out his name.

By the time she came back to herself, he had a
condom in his hand and was about to sheathe himself.

"Let me. I didn't get a chance to touch you and I
need to."

He hesitated then handed her the square packet.
She unwrapped the condom, but before she rolled it
on him, she gripped his thick cock in her hand. Now
she knew what velvet and steel felt like, she mused as
she pumped up and down his shaft.

A low growl erupted from his throat, and she in-
wardly smiled at the fact that she could make this big
man react with such intensity.

She brushed the pre-come off the head and he
drew in a harsh breath.

"Keep playing and you won't get to know what it
feels like to have me inside you," he warned her.

"Now that would be a shame." Because she really
did want the experience of feeling him in her body this
one time. Her heart gave a kick at the limiting thought.
Pushing it aside, she covered his shaft with protection.

And then he took control. Once again, he spread her thighs, this time making room for himself between her legs.

"I don't think I can go slow," he said, those indigo-blue eyes almost black.

"I don't want you to." No, she wanted to feel him, hard and strong inside her, now, and again tomorrow when she had to put this behind her. She didn't ever want to forget.

He met her gaze, thrust deep, and she felt him everywhere. He didn't take it slow nor did he hesitate. He began to move, and she soared to heights she'd never experienced before or even dreamed of. If this was great sex, then she'd been seriously missing out. Compared to this, she'd never even had good sex.

He rocked into her, his gaze on hers, never breaking eye contact, and that was what made this so different. And—dare she even think it?—special.

He dipped his head, his mouth capturing hers in a kiss as he ground his body against hers, and she was lost. All she could do was feel.

Austin inside her.

Austin taking her harder.

Austin consuming her.

Owning her.

And then she was coming so hard she saw stars. Her body was his to do with as he pleased, and somehow he stretched her orgasm out, utter bliss dominating her, as he stiffened and came, not on a shout but with her name on his lips.

*   *   *

Quinn lay beside Austin. He inhaled and exhaled, trying to catch his breath while she did the same. His fingers tangled in the strands of her hair, as if he couldn't not touch her. Or maybe that's what she wanted to think. After feeling him inside her body, she knew he was different from anyone she'd been with in the past. It hurt, knowing she wasn't the right woman for him.

"I have a proposition for you," he said, still twirling her hair around his finger, the tug on her scalp innocently arousing.

"You want me to think after that orgasm scrambled my brains?" she murmured, still foggy. "What is it?" She rolled to the side, giving herself a view of his incredibly sculpted naked body.

Football might be behind him, but he still worked out, kept himself in shape. Reaching out, she drew circles on his skin as she touched his chest, noticing that his cock started to get hard again. She blinked at his obvious stamina and realized by the tiny pulsing between her thighs she was ready to go again, too.

"Stay in my bed. Be with me until it's time for you

to go," he said in a gruff voice.

Her hand stilled as his words took her off guard. She opened then closed her mouth. "I—"

"There's really no reason to say no. We're living under the same roof. We want each other. And when you go home, we can go back to our regular lives. We've already crossed that line, Quinn. Why not enjoy each other?"

Because this one time had already spoiled her for all other men? Because it was already going to be hard enough to get over him? Because the more often they were together like this, the harder it would be to go to work and see him every day?

From her room across the hall, she heard her cell phone ring, giving her an out she desperately needed. She wasn't ready to answer him now. "That's my phone."

She started to roll to the other side of the mattress, but he wrapped his arm around her waist. "Wait. Let it go to voicemail."

It didn't matter because the ringing stopped. "Austin, if we keep this up, someone is going to get hurt." Namely her.

He buried his face in the crook of her neck and licked the tendon there, then bit down with his teeth. Her entire body spasmed in reaction. Even her thighs squeezed together, causing a near mini orgasm to take hold.

"Yeah? Says who? I won't hurt you, Quinn. Giving in to what we want makes sense."

His deep voice rumbled in her ear. *Do it*, the part of her that wanted both orgasms and as much time as she could get with him urged. They had a short window together. Why not make the most of it?

But this was so not smart, she argued against it with much less force.

He slid his hand around her waist and dipped his fingers between her thighs. "Tell me again why this is a bad idea?" he asked, toying with her clit and arousing her easily.

She moaned and parted her legs to make room for his hand. "Fine," she said, rolling onto her side. "While I'm here, I'll stay in your room and we can ... do this."

And as he grabbed another condom from the nightstand, sheathed himself, and raised her leg, entering her slowly and deliberately from behind, she knew she was in so much trouble.

After another round of incredible sex, a shared pepperoni pizza, and a phone call to her cousin, Amy, who was thrilled to have a babysitting job, Quinn felt like maybe things were falling into place in a way she could handle.

If she kept her emotions tightly locked away and

allowed herself to be with Austin, allowed herself to enjoy the short times she would have with Jenny once Amy arrived tomorrow, and didn't obsess or worry about the future or messy things like emotions, then this would be the perfect situation. And in a few days, her life would go back to normal.

Right.

*　　*　　*

Early the next morning, Austin answered the door to a girl who reminded him very much of a younger version of Quinn. From her dark hair to her green eyes, the family genes were strong.

"You must be Amy," he said to the girl in jeans, a Miami Thunder tee shirt, and a bright smile on her face. Apparently Quinn hadn't been kidding when she said her family loved sports.

"Hi, Mr. Prescott."

He smiled. "Call me Austin and come on in. Quinn is with Jenny. That's my…" He choked and said, "Daughter." Dammit, he wished he knew for sure.

Amy followed him in and he led her to Quinn. Jenny was swinging, the equipment set up between the family room and the kitchen so they could keep an eye on her whichever room they were in.

"Oh my gosh, look at her! She's so cute!" Amy

knelt down by the swing, stopped the motion, and immediately began to make cooing noises at the baby. Jenny gurgled back, doing her best little smile.

Quinn shot him a look as if to say *see?*

"Thank you," he said, walking up to her. Out of respect for her family, he didn't wrap his arm around her the way he wanted to. "This is going to be amazing. I can feel it."

She grinned. "This is what the Stone girls are trained for," she said wryly.

"What's her schedule like?" Amy had walked up behind him and joined them.

Quinn hugged her cousin before she pointed to a notepad. "Okay, so she had her bottle at six this morning. She should be good until between eleven and twelve and then again between five and six, depending on timing. We'll be home by six thirty."

Amy nodded. "No problem."

"Bottles are premade in the fridge. You're good for the day. Diapers are upstairs in her room. Right now she's in a pack and play," Quinn said, opening the refrigerator to show Amy the bottles lined up in the door. She didn't explain the reasons Jenny didn't have a real crib, for which Austin was grateful.

"Easy enough. Can I use the instant hot to heat the bottle?" Amy pointed to the faucet on the side of the sink.

"There's actually a bottle warmer. Whichever is easier for you. You know the drill. Make sure it's not too hot. Clothing changes are in the drawers in Jenny's room. If there's a real mess, I'll show you where the laundry room is. Don't forget to use the Dreft," Quinn said, to which Amy rolled her eyes.

Glancing at Austin, the young girl laughed. "She forgets that I'm already babysitting my older sister's kid when she and her husband go out on date night. I know the drill. We all know the drill." She looked at Quinn. "Show me the rooms. I can handle everything else."

"Okay, but also, for changing her diaper, Jenny gets fussy if the wipes are cold. We use a warmer, so make sure they're a comfortable temperature."

Amy nodded. "No problem."

"Oh! And since you can drive, in an emergency and only in an emergency, the truck with the car seat is in the garage." She'd asked Austin about that earlier this morning. "Emergencies are sudden spikes in raging high fever and meeting us at the doctor. That's all."

"I know, Quinn. You can trust me," Amy said solemnly.

Quinn nodded. "She's just so tiny and precious."

Quinn walked over to the swing and stopped it long enough to give Jenny a smacking kiss on her cheek that had the baby giggling, causing Austin's heart to squeeze inside his chest.

His brain already spun from the list of things Quinn had given her cousin, most of which he'd have forgotten if he'd done the explaining himself. He was sure he'd have only remembered to tell Amy to make sure she fed Jenny. Once again, he looked at Quinn with utter admiration and something more.

Something he couldn't afford to think about or name.

He might be sleeping with her and unable to be in the same room with her without wanting her, but the fact that she was so smart, so innately caring about the baby chipped away at his heart.

After Quinn gave Amy a tour of the house, showed her everything she might need for the baby, and reminded her of the instructions she'd already given, they were able to leave for the office.

He took the Porsche, and enclosed in the small space of the car, he inhaled her musky, arousing scent and hoped it remained there for a long time.

"Your cousin reminds me of you," he said as they pulled off the highway near the office.

"In what way?" Quinn shifted in her seat, her skirt lifting and revealing a nice expanse of knee and upper leg.

"Well, other than looks, she's as competent, serious, and devoted to her job as you are."

"You could tell all that in one meeting?" Quinn asked, sounding amused.

"She didn't appreciate you reminding her of everything you'd already told her, she didn't appear fazed by the possibility of dirty baby laundry, which we both know means vomit or..." He shook his head, not wanting to think about *that*. "And she didn't flinch when you said the word *emergency*."

Basically, though, because Quinn trusted Amy, so did Austin. "I figure you know what you're doing when it comes to Jenny, and you wouldn't have suggested Amy if she wasn't the right choice."

"I appreciate your faith in me. But Amy is smart and capable. And you know I'll check in on her. Often."

"Careful, I might think you have a soft spot for Jenny," he said, chuckling.

"You know I do." Her voice turned low and serious.

And a part of him wished that meant more than it actually did.

*   *   *

With a great babysitter in Amy, the next few days passed in a blur of Quinn catching up on work and things getting back to normal at the office. If she missed the baby's sweet smell and adorable face, she refused to admit it to anyone, especially herself. And her nights were spent, as agreed, in Austin's bed, which wasn't a hardship.

He was seductive and completely attentive to her needs. The man knew his way around her body, and she'd had more orgasms than she'd had in a lifetime combined. She'd spent the last week living a life she'd sworn she didn't want, taking care of an infant, and the last three nights in bed with a man she couldn't resist.

As if she'd conjured him with her thoughts, Austin stepped out of his office. Although she'd just seen him this morning, she was struck anew at how handsome he was. In his normal slacks and dress shirt, sleeves rolled up, exposing his forearms, and with the sexy light beard on his face, she was reminded of what that scruff felt like against her skin. Rubbing her face, scratching her thighs. When she breathed in, the scent of him overwhelmed her in the best possible way.

"Quinn?"

"Yes?" She blinked, realizing she'd been staring and then daydreaming, and in that time, he'd sat down on the edge of her desk.

A knowing smile lifted his lips, showing her a small dimple in his cheek she only noticed up close. "I asked you if Amy can babysit tomorrow night. Paul was supposed to attend the sports journalist banquet, but he asked if I'd handle this one, and I'd like you to go with me."

As his date or as his assistant, she wondered, unable to judge by the hot look in his eyes as he met her gaze. She had no intention of asking. "Of course I will. Amy already works for you during the weekend days. I'm sure she won't mind staying, but I'll call her now. Dress code?" she asked.

"Black tie."

She nodded. "Got it. I'll have to go home and pick up an outfit." She had a handful of dresses she'd bought in the time she'd been working for Austin for occasions such as these. And then it dawned on her. "Actually, your mom is coming home today, isn't she? I'll be back in my own home by tomorrow."

His hand froze midway to his face. This was a discussion they hadn't had. A topic they'd deftly avoided. Her because she really did like the time she'd spent with Austin, and him probably because it meant he'd have to handle the baby more by himself, unless his mother moved in.

He actually looked hurt by the notion, yet that was the agreement.

"In that case, I'll pick you up on the way," he said abruptly and rose from his seat. "I'll let you get back to work." He walked back into his office and shut the door without looking back.

She told herself she was relieved her time as a pseudo-nanny was coming to an end, and a part of her even believed it. Just not all of her and that truth really concerned her. Worst of all, she couldn't help feeling like she'd disappointed him somehow.

She swallowed hard and put the thought out of her head, getting back to work.

The rest of the day passed quietly. Austin took calls in his office, and she handled the phone and clients from her desk.

Then, knowing she had to make a good impression on Saturday, she decided to treat herself but she didn't want to go alone. Picking up her cell, she pulled up her best friend's number. A friend whose calls she'd been avoiding since Friday night, because how did she explain her current situation and have it make sense?

Evie Wolfe was a private investigator, and like Quinn, she came from a large family. Unlike Quinn, Evie was the only girl with four brothers who drove her insane and vice versa. Because how could her macho brothers keep up their overprotective behavior with a sister who was a PI, had self-defense skills, and could take care of herself?

At the thought, Quinn grinned. She missed seeing her best friend. She pressed Evie's name.

After one ring, her friend's voice sounded loud and

clear. "Where the hell have you been?"

Quinn sighed. "You wouldn't believe it if I told you."

"Well, you're going to. It isn't like you not to call me back. Why have you been avoiding me?" Evie asked.

She was going to have to explain to her friend eventually. "Can you spend the day with me tomorrow and I'll tell you everything? Hair, mani-pedi, and for me, makeup because I have an event that night."

"Ooh, sounds like fun! I'll pick you up. Let me know what time."

Quinn smiled. "I'm looking forward to it, too. I'll make the appointments and get back to you."

"Sounds good."

After hanging up, Quinn called the salon and booked a full day of appointments for herself and Evie. Luckily, there was a makeup artist on-site so she didn't have to go anywhere afterwards for a makeover.

She blew out a breath and sighed. There, she thought. She was getting back to taking care of herself.

Tapping a pen against the desk, she picked up her phone again and this time dialed her cousin. "Amy? How's Jenny?" she asked, unable not to worry about the little girl who wasn't hers.

*　　*　　*

Quinn had left for her spa day to get ready for tonight, and Jenny had fallen asleep again after her bottle. Austin lay down on his bed and groaned just as his cell rang and his mother's name flashed on the screen.

As much as he was glad his mom was home, he couldn't ignore the disappointment that flowed through him, knowing it meant the end of his time with Quinn.

He tapped on his mom's name and took the call. "Hi, Mom! How was your trip?"

"Oh, honey, it was wonderful. Seeing all those old friends was truly so much fun."

"As if you're old," he said with a laugh. But at her nasal tone of voice, he narrowed his gaze. "Are you sick?"

"That's why I'm calling. I have the worst cold known to mankind. You know those ships with the close quarters. Bugs and viruses travel fast. I woke up with it this morning and I have no idea how long it's going to last." At that, she coughed and he knew for sure she wasn't coming around Jenny.

"Feel better, Mom. Rest. I'll check on you tomorrow."

"Thanks, honey. Give that baby a kiss for me. I heard from your sister and she said that you and Quinn are managing well. That takes a load off my mind. Love you." She disconnected the call, and though he hated that his mother was sick, a slow smile took hold because Quinn wouldn't be going anywhere after all.

At least not yet.

Chapter Seven

Quinn soaked her toes in the warm, soapy water as the massage chair behind her pressed into her tight muscles. Beside her, Evie did the same. She'd already had her hair trimmed and blow-dried, her nails were done in a French manicure, and after her pedicure, she'd have her makeup done.

Though she had a book opened on her Kindle, Evie was not going to let Quinn read. Or ignore the conversation she wanted to have. She'd been peppering Quinn with questions since she'd explained the situation with Austin.

"So you've been living with your boss?" Evie asked, not moderating her tone.

Quinn's friend had long dark hair, olive skin, a beautiful complexion, and a very loud voice. The women doing their toes glanced up at Quinn, but neither said a word and they went back to work.

Quinn leaned closer to Evie's seat. "Shh. Yes, I am staying with Austin. Just to help with the baby." *And sleep in his bed, don't forget that*, she thought, keeping the personal information to herself. Evie would have a field day lecturing her if she let it slip.

Evie narrowed her chocolate-brown gaze. "So let me get this straight. The boss whose kiss you liked now has a baby, and you're helping to take care of her while living in his house." Thank God she'd decided to whisper. "You, Quinnlyn Stone, who swore off children and any jobs dealing with kids and babies? Have I got my facts straight?"

Quinn gripped the armrests harder in her hands. "You know you do. So why are you repeating everything I already told you?"

"Because it's insane, that's why. I don't understand. Why can't the rich man just hire a nanny?" Evie glanced at her toes and wriggled them before looking up at the nail tech. "Excuse me. I hate to do this but can we switch to a brighter coral?"

The woman nodded. "I'll go get a few colors for you to choose from."

"Thanks." Evie smiled in gratitude.

"You're a pain in the ass." Quinn had chosen a pale pink. She didn't need her toes standing out at the event tonight.

Evie shrugged. "I like bright colors. So sue me. When does this part of your job come to an end?"

"Later today," she said, ignoring the pang in her chest. "His mother is back from her cruise." She and Austin hadn't done any talking last night, and she'd rushed out this morning so she didn't know Christine's plans.

"But things settled in this week. He hired my cousin Amy to babysit so we had someone during the day. Work got easier. I'm not wearing Jenny hanging from my chest anymore." She smiled at the memory of the sweet baby smell when she'd lean down with the baby tight against her. "And Amy will watch her while we go to the banquet tonight and…" At the dumb-struck look on Evie's face, Quinn's voice trailed off. "What's wrong?"

Evie glanced at the three different colors on her toes and picked the one she liked best before looking back at Quinn. "I thought I heard you discussing wearing a baby like it was no big deal."

Quinn pulled her bottom lip between her teeth and released it with a pop. "It isn't a big deal. I was doing Austin a favor. The man was completely at a loss. Now he's not a pro but he can really handle the baby better. It's really cute to watch."

"I'll bet it is," Evie muttered with a smirk on her face. "Hot ex-football player taking care of a tiny baby. Has all the makings of a Hallmark movie with a happy ending if the heroine wasn't so anti-baby."

Quinn shook her head and groaned for good measure. "Be quiet and quit reading into things." She glanced away because she knew Evie would see too much. Like her growing feelings for Austin and Jenny.

"So let's talk about you. Are you over what that jackass John did to you?"

She glanced at the light leather jacket Evie wore all the time. A woman had hired Evie to follow the husband she suspected of cheating. That husband had turned out to be John, who had lashed out physically at Evie when he'd realized she would cost him his family.

Evie frowned. "You know that subject is not up for discussion."

Quinn reached out and squeezed her friend's hand. "Someday it will be. You'll need to talk about it and I'll be there." Because the incident had shattered Evie's confidence in her own judgment and she'd need to get over it to do her job. "You aren't still drowning your sorrows in chocolate fudge ice cream, are you?" Quinn lightened the subject.

"Because of that jerk? No. But I'll never turn down chocolate. Speaking of, want a Hershey's kiss?" Evie reached into her oversized bag and pulled out a handful of chocolate.

Quinn grinned and accepted a kiss. By tomorrow, Christine would take over baby duty. Quinn would move back home, and these silver candies were the only kisses she'd be receiving. At that thought, she sunk deeper into the massage chair and sighed.

Her cell rang and she saw it was Austin. "Hello?" she asked, answering the call.

"Hi. So I have something to tell you."

She stiffened in her seat. "Is Jenny okay?"

Her words caught Evie's attention and she unabashedly leaned in to listen. Quinn rolled her eyes.

"Jenny's fine," he said and she relaxed. "Then what's wrong?"

"Well, my mother called, and she picked up a really bad cold on the cruise so she can't come help out. Yet."

"I see."

At her deliberately bland tone, Evie raised her eyebrow in curiosity.

"I'm sorry, Quinn. I know you're looking forward to getting back to your life."

She drew a deep breath. "I'll stay," she said. "But I have to go. I'm in the middle of a manicure." She disconnected the call and refused to look too deeply into how she was feeling about the unexpected change in plans.

She'd thought she'd be going home to her own bed for the first time in a week. Instead she was going to maintain the status quo. So why did she feel so relieved instead of disappointed?

* * *

Austin waited for Quinn to meet him downstairs to head over to the Fortieth Annual Joe Matthis Awards Dinner. Matthis had been a quarterback for the Miami Thunder during a particularly spectacular ten-year run years ago. The event benefitted the Miami Special Needs Foundation, which was a fundraising, grant-raising entity that supported programs for children and adults who had intellectual and developmental disabilities in Miami. In essence, the foundation protected benefit eligibility and had been founded by Joe Matthis himself.

The Miami Thunder players would be there, along with Ian and his wife and members of the press. Austin would be proud to have Quinn on his arm and not just as his assistant.

He'd broken the news to her about his mother's illness and she'd said two words that sent relief rushing through him. *I'll stay.* And though he sensed she was fighting herself, enjoying her time with him and Jenny more than she wanted to admit, he wouldn't press her to say it out loud. He'd just take one day at a time.

Meanwhile, he hoped to have the DNA test results early next week, which would either cement his future with Jenny or put him in the awful position of deciding what to do with the infant who had grown on him in the short week she'd been in his home.

A rustle of noise sounded, and he turned to look

up the circular staircase in time to see Quinn descend wearing a red floor-length dress, and damn if that wasn't her color. The material draped around her body and up one shoulder, leaving both arms bare.

His dick perked up at the sight of her, her beautiful face made-up, smoky eyes lined in black, and lipstick matching her dress.

As she reached the bottom step, he let out a low whistle. "You're gorgeous."

A light flush rose to her cheeks. "Thank you." She stepped up to him and pulled on either side of his bowtie. "You're pretty hot yourself, Mr. Prescott." In her high heels, she didn't have to lift onto her tiptoes to lean in and press a kiss on one side of his mouth, then the other.

"Marking me?" he asked with a grin, lifting a hand to wipe his mouth in case she'd left red marks. He couldn't walk into the banquet with lipstick on him.

"Actually it's long-wear and smudge-proof. You're safe."

Looking at the seductress in the formfitting dress, he wasn't so sure.

*   *   *

Quinn watched Austin schmoozing businessmen, athletes, and reporters, struck by how at ease he was with a variety of different types of people. How much others gravitated toward him, men and women alike. And while he did his thing, he kept a strong arm around her waist, hanging on to her as if she were his date and not his assistant.

She refused to overthink anything about his actions or her emotions or how good she felt against his hard, hot body. Instead she enjoyed the night. How could she not when Austin in a tuxedo took her breath away? His scruff, a permanent fixture, made him sexier than if he were clean-shaven. And his masculine scent was not only a turn-on but it reminded her of the nights she spent tangled in his arms. The fact that she knew she'd end the evening in his bed made the mingling part of this event more bearable.

"Austin?" an unfamiliar voice called.

He turned. "Alex! Good to see you!"

The two men embraced with a quick hug and slap on the back. "Alex Dare, this is my … assistant, Quinn Stone. Quinn, my cousin Alex." The word *cousin* slid smoothly off his tongue. He really had adapted to his new reality.

She looked at the handsome man, giving him a warm smile. His brown hair and matching eyes made for a striking combination, and like Austin, his muscular frame filled out his tuxedo.

"Hi, Alex. Nice to meet you." She knew this was Ian Dare's half brother.

"Same here. And this is my wife, Madison."

A pretty woman with blonde hair and blue eyes grinned back. "Hi, Austin. It's been awhile. Hello, Quinn. Nice to meet you, too."

Austin chuckled, the sound low and deep, settling in Quinn's stomach.

"Well, you two and your many kids, your traveling for the Thunder ... keeps you busy," Austin said. He glanced at Quinn. "Alex and Madison run a foundation for the Thunder that teaches athletes how to prepare for life after football. Especially those with concussion issues and CTE," he said of the brain injury that was debilitating for many football players and was only diagnosed postmortem.

She nodded. "I've read a lot about your work. I think it's wonderful. And Madison, it's great to meet you. I also heard about your foster kids. What you two do ... it's just amazing." Madison and her husband took in foster children who needed homes. Some they adopted, some they kept until they moved on. Whatever was best for the children. She'd heard Ian mention it more than once.

Madison smiled. "We love our kids and our lives. And it was cool to discover there were more Dares," she said to Austin, a grin on her pretty face.

"Well, well. Everyone is here." Ian Dare joined them, his wife, Riley, by his side.

"Look at us, one big, happy family. Should I say we've come a long way?" Alex asked, letting out a laugh.

Riley, a pretty brunette, rolled her eyes. "How about not?"

Apparently the Dare family dynamic was unique on all sides. Sperm donation for the Prescotts, and Paul's brother, Robert, had two families at the same time. It had taken Ian awhile to accept Alex and his siblings, but they were now close, according to Austin.

"Always the wiseass," Ian muttered. "I'd worry if you changed."

Everyone laughed.

The night went on, the Dare family mingling more than not, everyone friendly to Quinn. She liked Ian's and Alex's wives, and they went out of their way to be open, warm, and genuine. Given Quinn's experience with many of the sports wives, Madison and Riley were a welcome change.

Quinn excused herself to go to the ladies' room and, when she finished, made her way back to the bar area, needing a glass of water for her dry throat.

"Quinn? Is that you?" a familiar voice called, and a frisson of unease wrapped its way around her. She turned. "Daniel, hello." She faced her ex-fiancé, who stood in his tux, an arm around an attractive woman with dark hair and the beginnings of a pregnant belly.

She swallowed hard.

"Hi, Quinn. I thought that was you."

She smiled at him. "Yes, this is an event that's part of my job. What are you doing here?" Last she'd heard, college professors didn't come to sporting foundation events.

"My wife, Kelly, is a reporter and she's here for work, too," he said proudly.

"Is this Quinn, as in your ex-fiancée?" Kelly asked.

Daniel cleared his throat. "It is. Kelly, this is Quinnlyn Stone."

"It's nice to meet you," Quinn murmured.

Before they could continue, Austin had joined her, easily slipping in beside her and wrapping an arm firmly around her waist. "What did I miss?" he asked, eyeing her ex and his wife.

Quinn wondered if Austin had caught an expression that indicated she wasn't overly comfortable. She'd meant to hide her feelings, but coming face-to-face with Daniel and his pregnant wife had been a surprise. She didn't begrudge him happiness, but she hadn't seen him in so long, this meeting was awkward for her.

"Who is this?" Daniel asked, his gaze on Austin.

"Austin Prescott." He extended his hand and Daniel took it. "I'm Quinn's…"

"Boss," she chimed in.

"And you are?" Austin asked.

"Daniel Munroe. Quinn's ex." Daniel grinned sheepishly, pulling his wife closer to his side.

"They were engaged," Kelly said, her voice tight.

Beside her, Austin stiffened. He didn't know about her engagement and why should he? She'd ended it just before she'd gotten the job at Dare Nation, and they'd been colleagues for the past year. Not friends. Certainly not lovers, at least not until this past week. She'd had no reason to get into her past.

Wanting to keep things light, Quinn glanced at Kelly. "I hear congratulations are in order. My brother told me you're expecting."

At her curious glance, Quinn explained, "Matt is a professor at the college with Daniel."

"Right," Kelly said. "I forgot that."

"Do you want to see pictures of the baby's sonogram?" If Daniel had had a particularly annoying fault, it had been that he was clueless to other people's discomfort or emotions. Which was probably why he'd thought Quinn would change her mind and want to have his baby one day when she'd made her feelings perfectly clear.

Kelly shifted uncomfortably on her feet. "I don't think they want to see—"

"Of course we want to look," Quinn said. She didn't want Kelly to view her as a threat of any kind.

Daniel pulled the picture from his wallet, and they spent the next few minutes oohing and aahing over the black-and-white blob.

Finally, Kelly spoke up. "My feet hurt. Can we go sit down now?" She tugged on her husband's arm.

Catching on, Daniel nodded. "Sure. It was nice seeing you again, Quinn. Good to meet you, too," he said to a silent Austin.

Finally and blessedly they were left alone and Quinn let out a relieved breath. "God, was Daniel that obtuse when I was with him?" She shook her head, laughing until she caught sight of Austin's stony face. "What's wrong?"

"You were engaged?"

"I was. Yes." And she didn't want to discuss her past here. "Is it time to go home? If we're going to dig into my old relationships, I'd like to do it in private."

He inclined his head and took her elbow, leading her out of the ballroom.

She didn't know what his problem was but she intended to find out. Except he didn't make it easy.

He hadn't said a word since they agreed to leave. Not when they waited for his Porsche to be brought around by the valet. Not on the drive home. And not when they walked into the house and she checked in with Amy and let her cousin out, locking up for the night. And not when she walked into the bedroom and closed the door behind her.

Clearly something was going through his mind. Walking up behind him, she wrapped her arms around his waist and placed her cheek against his back. He'd already removed his jacket, so she leaned against his shirt, not worrying if she transferred makeup to the white material. "Austin? What's bothering you?"

"Nothing. I'm fine," he said curtly.

"Liar." Her body moved against him as she laughed quietly. "You're jealous for no reason."

"Why did you break up?" he asked, not denying her accusation.

She kept them entangled together when she spoke. "When Daniel and I got engaged, we agreed that we didn't want kids, but come to find out, he thought he could convince me to change my mind. I just... I didn't want children with him. So we broke up."

"And you have no feelings left for him? Because when they walked up to you, the look on your face..."

She shook her head and turned him around to face her. "None at all." She felt more for Austin than she ever had for Daniel, but how did she admit that when they had to have an end date? "But I have lots of feelings for you." In the end, she couldn't deny him knowing that she cared.

"I spent the night watching you in that dress and wanted nothing more than to peel it off you," he said in a gruff voice.

She turned the side where the zipper was under her arm. "Then do it."

He reached out and slid the zipper down slowly, careful with the thin material and watching out for her skin. Once he'd freed her from confinement, she shrugged off the one shoulder and let the dress slide to the floor.

His hot gaze raked over her, taking in her matching red thong and barely there strapless bra. "Fuck," he said as he adjusted his cock.

She grinned. "Uncomfortable? Then take them off."

Without waiting for him to act first, she unhooked the button, unzipped the fly, and eased the slacks over his hips, taking his boxer briefs with them. Then, keeping her eyes on his, she knelt down and took his cock in her hand.

He groaned as she wrapped her hands around the thick shaft and slid her hand up and down his erection. "You didn't let me finish last time. Are you going to deny me the chance tonight?" she asked, licking him like the most delicious treat.

His hand came to rest on her head. She opened her mouth and took him in. The next few minutes happened in what felt like slow motion. Her sliding him deep into her throat, guiding him out, in and out until he took over the motion himself. His hips pumped back and forth, and he was in control, all but fucking her mouth.

Her knees rubbed against the carpet, her hands gripped his thighs, and soon he was coming, long spurts down her throat. She swallowed quickly, accepting all of him until he pulled out and she nearly collapsed to the floor.

*   *   *

Austin drew in deep breaths, recovering from the most intense orgasm of his life. When he could breathe, he leaned down, lifted Quinn into his arms, and laid her down on his bed. Her eyes gleamed with the satisfaction of a job well done, and he smiled at her, shaking his head.

"Liked that, did you?" he asked.

Her lips were still red from the non-smudge lipstick and she grinned. "So what if I did?"

He pressed his mouth to hers, not caring that she tasted like him. He only wanted to devour this woman who had crept into the deep recesses of his soul. Parts he hadn't known existed but now had to face.

He'd never cared what a female he slept with did in her past, her present, or with whom. But when he'd found out Daniel Munroe was Quinn's ex-fiancé, an unfamiliar emotion had flowed through him, thick, molten, and ugly. Quinn had pegged it tonight. But jealousy was a foreign feeling. No wonder he hadn't been able to pin it down at first, yet the word felt right to describe the pain in his chest. The hole in his gut. The desire to keep her by his side and not let another man even look her way.

And when she'd told him she'd ended things with Daniel because she hadn't wanted children and he had, something inside Austin had broken. It made him want to own her while he could, make her his, ruin her for all other men.

The kiss turned hot and hungry quickly, and he rolled to his back, pulling her on top of him. He wanted to see her face when she clasped him inside her body and watch her expression when she came. His cock rubbed against her damp sex and desire ricocheted through him.

He paused only long enough to grab a condom and cover himself before he braced his hands on the mattress and raised himself above her, his dick poised at her entrance. Then he began to slowly push his way inside.

His gaze never left her face, and when he locked eyes with her, she didn't waver, either. He watched her as he made her his, filling her up, joining them completely. "Do you feel me?" he asked, rising and thrusting into her again.

She moaned and nodded. "And I need more. Harder. Please," she said and lifted her legs and wrapped them around him, locking her ankles behind his back.

He couldn't deny her anything. He didn't want to. With a groan, he continued to thrust deep, in and out, harder with each slam of his hips into hers. He did his best to hold her gaze, but as desire ramped up, his stare grew fuzzy. His balls drew up and a familiar tingle zipped up his spine.

"Oh God." She grabbed his shoulders, her fingernails digging into his skin.

The pain ratcheted up his need, but he wanted her to come first and that he needed to see. He took a hand, slid it between them, and glided his finger over her slick clit.

"Yes, there." She arched her hips, a sob escaping her lips.

He pressed harder and triggered her release, her body arching into him. Cheeks flushed, lips parted, eyes closed, she looked like a goddess beneath him, calling out his name as she came.

He waited, holding on as he ground into her as she rode out her orgasm, only letting himself go when she was through. He picked up his pace, but it only took three more hard thrusts before he came harder than he ever had before, releasing inside her.

He collapsed on top of her, breathing in the mixed scent of sweat on her skin and the sweet fragrance she'd used tonight. He inhaled, taking in her essence.

"Are you sniffing me?" she asked.

He let out a low chuckle. "I might be." He reached down and tickled her sides, causing her to giggle before he rolled off her, separating them and definitely feeling the loss.

"I'm going to get rid of the condom," he said, rolling to the side and putting his feet on the floor.

He headed to the bathroom and cleaned up, returning just as she sighed, stretching her lithe body out on the bed.

"God, that was good," she murmured.

"Just good?" He lay back down by her side, looking into her eyes.

Her expression softened. "No, it wasn't just good. It was incredible," she murmured, reaching out and running her hand over his cheek.

Thank God. Because it had been a life-altering experience for him. Quinn wasn't just a good fuck. Hell, she wasn't even a passing fling. He wanted her in his life for good. He just knew better than to think he could keep her.

*   *   *

After Quinn fell asleep, Austin rose and walked out of

the bedroom. He flipped on the hall light and stepped into Jenny's room. A night-light lit the room and, along with the hallway glow, gave him a good view of the baby.

She slept on her back, as Quinn had explained to him was necessary, and every so often, little baby sounds escaped from her mouth. She was perfection, from her flawless skin to her tiny nose. Even so, he made a mental note to make an appointment with a pediatrician and have her looked at. The first week had been too full of adjustments for him to have even thought of taking her to a doctor for a checkup. But he wanted to make certain she was as healthy as she appeared.

He drew in a deep breath, watching her sleep, and a warm feeling flowed through him, settled in his chest, and remained. He stayed for a good twenty minutes, aware of the thoughts going through his head, what they meant for his life and his future, waiting for a feeling of panic to surface. None did.

And as he headed back to his room and settled in with Quinn, pulling her into his arms, he was still sure he planned on doing the right thing. Even if it cost him the woman he was certain he loved.

* * *

Quinn rose to the sound of the baby crying. She

paused for a brief moment, cataloguing the good aches and pains in her body. She'd even woken up in the middle of the night to find Austin's head between her thighs, his mouth on her sex, his tongue toying with her clit. He'd been voracious. She'd been his plaything, and all he'd cared about was her pleasure.

She moaned at the memory and Jenny cried once more.

Austin lifted his head and met her gaze.

"Diaper or bottle?" she asked the usual question.

That had been their routine. One of them would choose who took what job and they did it. Together.

"Bottle," he said.

She knew he'd become an expert at either making one from scratch or warming it up from the fridge, and she was impressed with his new skill. In fact, she doubted he even needed her to help anymore, whether his mother was back or not, but she was reluctant to bring up the question. She wasn't ready to leave him just yet. Soon. But right now she wanted to enjoy what little time she had left.

"I'll get her." Quinn pulled on one of Austin's tee shirts and walked barefoot to the baby's room. Austin headed for the kitchen.

"Hey, little girl. Good morning." Sunlight had just begun to stream through the blinds, and Jenny's little face looked up at her. "Are you ready for the whole family to descend for football Sunday?"

According to Austin, it was a family tradition to watch the games together whenever they could when Damon or Jaxon was playing. Damon was at the end of preseason and he probably wouldn't play much. The teams tended to protect their better players, keeping them unhurt until the season officially began, but he'd told Austin he expected to have some playing time. But Jaxon would be on the field.

Quinn picked Jenny up and cuddled her against one shoulder. "Austin's mom will be here if she's better, and his uncle Paul and Ron. Bri is coming, too. You remember Bri, right?" She babbled to the baby and walked to the small makeshift changing table they'd put together on the dresser. "I think I'll call Evie and invite her, too." Quinn wouldn't mind having her best friend by her side today.

"Let's change you, okay?" Quinn diapered the baby, the actions coming automatically and by rote.

She lifted Jenny and patted her little behind as they walked to the master bedroom, and she lay back on the mattress, propped against the pillows, keeping the baby in her arms.

Jenny smelled like baby powder and her shampoo. Closing her eyes, Quinn took in the sweet scent, torn by how much she already loved this child and how different a future she envisioned for herself. Even her feelings for Austin ran counter to what she'd been telling herself she needed from life for years. She wanted to be self-sufficient and have a career, not a family that demanded all her time and attention like her siblings and cousins had.

Thinking back over her teenage years, she remembered missing a date she'd been looking forward to because her niece had been sick, her uncle had been working, and her aunt turned to Quinn to watch her other kids. No one ever considered asking Quinn's siblings, and they had been younger. Quinn had always been, as Austin had called her, the baby whisperer. As for her canceled date, the guy had gone on to be with another girl he'd remained with throughout high school, and she heard they'd actually gotten married after college. Quinn had missed her chance.

Jenny gurgled and Quinn smiled. Even waiting for her morning bottle, Jenny was good. Once she was picked up, she tended to stop crying and wait for whatever came next, a diaper change or a bottle or her swing. She'd even adjusted to Austin, not shrieking whenever he came near. She was one of the most sweet-natured infants Quinn had ever encountered.

Austin walked back into the room, gray sweats riding low, showing off the vee on either side of his hips, his muscular chest bare and sexy. The bottle in his hand somehow merely added to his appeal.

He slid into the bed, and before she could hand the baby over, he scooped Jenny up, settling her into the crook of his arm and popping the bottle into her moving lips like a pro.

He grinned, obviously proud of himself. "I think she likes me."

Quinn laughed. "I'm pretty sure she's come around."

He looked down at the infant, a warm, adoring expression in his eyes. "I'm not giving her up," he said in a low, determined voice.

"What?" Quinn wasn't sure she'd heard him correctly.

He met her gaze. "If she's mine, obviously I'm going to fight for full custody. Hell, I want the bitch who abandoned her to sign away any legal rights. But I'm talking about if she's not mine. I'm not giving her up so some foster family can take her." He squared his shoulders, as if readying for a fight. "If she isn't mine by blood, she's mine now, and I'm going to make damn sure my lawyer does whatever he needs to do so I can keep her."

Quinn's heart thudded so loudly in her chest she could swear she heard the sound. "Oh, wow. I... Wow."

She hadn't seen this coming, although she should have. Despite faltering in the beginning, Austin had stepped up and taken care of Jenny, learning everything he could from Quinn. She'd even caught him reading up on babies on his laptop, not that she ever called him on it. She'd found it endearing.

"Austin, do you realize what you're in for?" she asked tentatively, not wanting to sound discouraging. "We're not just talking sleepless nights for a short time."

He nodded, his gaze somber and serious. "It's a lifetime commitment. A baby, a toddler, a kid, teenager... I know. And this may not be what I imagined for my future, but she's been given to me for a reason. And I'm keeping her." He pressed a kiss to the baby's head, as if to say, *and that's that.*

Quinn tried to swallow but her mouth had gone dry. A painful lump rose in her throat, because if she'd harbored any secret fantasies about being with Austin after the baby thing was settled, he'd just destroyed them with one brilliant, sweet, selfless decision.

Chapter Eight

"Quinnlyn Stone, why haven't you returned any of my calls?" Quinn's mother, Penelope, asked, her tone annoyed, over the phone.

Quinn sighed. "I've been tied up at work, and as you know, I'm helping out a friend with his baby. I've been busy," she said to her mother later Sunday morning.

As she spoke, she measured and put powder into the row of bottles on the counter in the kitchen. Austin had gone out to pick up food for the family, who would be here soon, and Jenny was in her swing.

"Yes, and I find that interesting considering you made it a point to tell me how much you didn't want to be a nanny or have your own children." Her mother's disappointment in Quinn's choices rang clear.

Although her mother had a career, she believed her children, her daughters in particular, should want to have babies. Lots of babies. Even if Penelope had turned baby duty over to her oldest.

Quinn blew out a breath. "You'll get grandchildren from Matthew, Chloe, or Jeff," she assured her mother. "I certainly wasn't going to leave Austin alone with a baby he didn't know how to take care of."

"Speaking of babies…" her mother began and Quinn stiffened, her shoulders tight with tension. "Matt mentioned that Daniel's wife is pregnant. You realize if you hadn't ended things, that could have been you, having his baby."

Closing her eyes, Quinn slowly counted to five before answering in an attempt to calm down. "And didn't you just say that I told you I didn't want kids? Maybe if you hadn't forced me to be everyone's babysitter, I'd have had more of my own life and wouldn't resent so much of my childhood," she said, her voice growing louder.

A gasp sounded and Quinn spun around, shocked to see Austin's mother standing in the kitchen.

Quinn blinked in surprise, at the same time, flushing with embarrassment at being overheard. "Mom, can we not rehash the past or argue? Listen, I need to go. I'll call you later," she said, softening her voice and disconnecting the call before her mother could reply.

She placed her phone on the counter and forced herself to look at Christine Prescott. "I'm so sorry you had to hear that."

The other woman appeared embarrassed, her cheeks flushed. "I knocked in case the baby was sleeping, but I didn't want to ring that loud bell. I just let myself in, which I probably shouldn't have done. I didn't mean to eavesdrop." She placed her handbag on a chair at the table. "But since I did hear ... are you okay?"

Quinn swallowed hard, ashamed she'd been caught arguing with her mother over things she usually kept inside. "It's nothing. I just—"

"Had an argument with your mom? Believe me, it happens." Christine walked across the room and took over with the bottles. "I've had more fights with my kids than I can remember. Prescotts are hardheaded," she said, and Quinn knew Christine was trying to lighten the mood. "Now that said, I take it being thrust into the role of caregiver for a baby was a trigger for you?"

Quinn sighed. "Come sit. You don't need to make formula. I've got it. Please." She put a hand on Christine's back and led her to the table and chairs.

Before they settled in, Christine stepped over to the baby, paused the swing, and brushed her fingers down Jenny's cheek. "Has she been good?"

"Yeah. She's delicious. Such a sweet baby." Quinn smiled. "And you're feeling better?" she asked Austin's mom.

"Much. Thank you."

Did that mean Christine planned to stay and help Austin, making Quinn an extra set of hands he no longer needed? She gripped the counter, surprised at the pang of *something* that went through her at the thought.

Christine lifted Jenny out of the swing and kept her cuddled against her as they sat down across from each other. "Now back to my question. I left for my cruise without really knowing what was going on here. Did I put you in a bad place?"

Had watching Jenny been a trigger? Quinn thought back to Christine's earlier question and sighed. "I come from a big family, and I was always good with the babies and the kids. The adults worked, and it fell to me to watch my siblings and cousins, which would have been fine except nobody ever stopped to wonder if they were interrupting anything in my life."

She closed her eyes at the memories. Friday nights with friends missed. Dates unimportant. "There were events I had to skip, assumptions made, and my parents even wanted me to become a full-time nanny instead of going to school." She pulled in a deep breath. "I adore kids but that's not the point."

Quinn waited for Austin's mother to criticize her for resenting the fact that she had to help out her family, but Christine's understanding smile knocked the wind out of her.

"Honey, when you have kids, they're your responsibility. I'm not judging your parents. I'm sure they had their reasons and did the best they could, but it wasn't your job to raise the other children in the family. And frankly it seems unfair of them to have asked it of you. Or not looked at what you wanted out of your own life."

Tears threatened to fall because of Austin's mother's innate understanding. When was the last time anyone had looked at Quinn and comprehended the basic fact that she'd just wanted her own life? To make her own choices?

"I love my parents, but I'm a little jealous of your kids right now," Quinn said, managing a smile.

Christine blushed and grinned. "Well, the way you stepped up and helped my son, I consider you family. So no need to be jealous. I'm here any time you need me." As she spoke, she patted Jenny's back.

"Thank you," Quinn murmured. "I should finish the bottles before Austin returns with all the sandwiches and food. The game starts in an hour." She didn't want to sit here and discuss her family's shortcomings and end up crying on this woman's shoulders.

"So about Jenny. Austin said there's been no word from her mother?" Christine obviously got the message and changed the subject.

Quinn shook her head. "No, and nothing from the private investigator, either." If his guys didn't get anywhere, she intended to offer up Evie's services.

Her friend was damn good at her job, even if she wasn't the top PI firm in Miami.

"What kind of woman abandons a baby and doesn't check in?" Christine asked, cuddling Jenny closer.

Since there was no answer to that question, Quinn merely shrugged.

"Can I take her into the family room?" Christine asked. "I saw a little blanket and a mobile hanging over it. I'll lay her down and let her play."

"Of course. Can I get you a cup of coffee or anything to drink or eat?" Quinn offered.

"I'm fine. You don't need to wait on me, honey." Christine rose from the chair with Jenny in her arms. "Come on, baby girl, let's get to know each other."

Quinn watched as the capable woman headed off with the baby. Now that Christine was feeling better and able to take care of Jenny, Quinn realized her time there was coming to an end, and she didn't like the way that made her feel.

*   *   *

Austin arrived home to a full house. He unloaded the subs and the bottles of soda, the chips, and the wings he'd picked up from his favorite place at the last minute. He loved Sunday football.

When he'd played, he'd given the sport his all. But

now he loved being a watcher and having a stake in the outcomes thanks to the players he agented.

He was glad to see his mom's car at the top of the drive, letting him know she was feeling better and up to seeing the baby. He hated when his mother got sick, but he didn't want Quinn to have an excuse to leave.

The bitch of it was, in just a week, he felt comfortable taking care of Jenny. He had the routine down pat, and she didn't scream at him anymore. Whether or not he wanted to handle her without Quinn was another story.

With the food in the house, everyone pitched in and helped set up. A little while later, Damon's game was on the big screen, the Miami Thunder playing in New York, and Jaxon's baseball game was on the smaller screen Austin used for dual games.

The doorbell rang and Austin went to answer it. So did Quinn and they met up in the entry hall.

"I invited my best friend," she said, reaching for the door and opening it.

"Quinn!" A woman with long almost-dark hair and tanned skin, wearing a Thunder jersey, pulled Quinn into a hug. "Thanks for inviting me." She stepped inside, her gaze going to Austin. "And this must be the man of the house?"

Quinn grinned. "Evie Wolfe, meet Austin Prescott, my boss and the baby's father," she said. Obviously

Evie knew the situation Quinn found herself in.

"It's nice to meet you." Evie held out her hand and he shook it. "He's hot," she said in an overly loud voice.

Quinn's cheeks flamed red. "Evie, you promised you'd behave," she chided her friend, then sheepishly glanced at Austin. "Evie speaks her mind."

Austin laughed. "Then I think I'll like her. Come on in," he said, gesturing inside the house to where the family had gathered.

They walked back to the family room and joined the others. Jenny had gone down for a nap in her room, the baby monitor on the table where they could keep an eye on her. And the women had congregated around the bar where the ice and soda choices were located. Austin watched as Quinn introduced Evie to Bri and her friend, Charlotte, a pretty woman with jet black hair, and they laughed and bonded over whatever women had in common. He was glad his family had embraced Quinn.

Paul walked up to him and wrapped an arm around his shoulder. He gestured to the couch where Ron sat, engrossed in both games on separate screens.

"How's it going?" Paul asked.

"It's going," Austin said of his life. "It's weird but I'm adjusting."

Paul nodded, leaning back against the oversized

cushion. "Ron and I opted not to have kids. We love to travel and we were close with you and your siblings. It was enough for us. But there is no doubt children can bring something wonderful to your life."

Austin glanced at the monitor and grinned. "Maybe if she'd continued to cry and scream at me all the time, I wouldn't have come around so fast. But Jenny makes it easy."

"And Quinn taught you everything you needed to know," his uncle said.

Austin let out a laugh. "You could more than say that."

"Have you thought about what I suggested? About going after what you want?" Paul asked, following Austin's gaze to where Quinn was laughing with the other women.

Austin rolled his shoulders. "I've thought about it a lot. Unfortunately I learned last night that Quinn broke up with her fiancé because he wanted kids and she didn't."

And it had hurt badly. Mostly because of the decision he'd made. "I'm going to fight for Jenny whether she's mine or not. Quinn not wanting kids is kind of a big barrier when the woman you love is finished raising other people's children."

And he did love her. His feelings for her had grown from the day they'd met, but this last week had shown him that Quinnlyn Stone was everything he desired in a partner.

His uncle looked to Quinn, who caught their gaze. Realizing they were talking about her, she flushed and glanced away. "Maybe she needs an adjustment period, too, but hers is just longer than yours. I see how she looks at you. Give it time."

Austin managed a nod because, really, what choice did he have?

"Now that your mother's feeling better, is Quinn going to move out?" Paul asked.

Austin's heart squeezed in his chest at the possibility. "I sure as hell hope not but that's been the promise all along." He hated the idea of going back to merely boss and assistant, never acknowledging the intense desire between them again.

"Look! Damon's in!" Ron gestured to the screen and the family gathered around to watch.

The screen was full movie-theater size, and Austin liked feeling as if he were on the field with every play. His brother had incredible talent and smarts as a quarterback, already earning six million dollars a year. They were banking on him reaching double digits in the next contract.

Austin watched the second quarter, keeping an eye on Damon. The Thunder were short on the first down. Austin leaned in closer. Quinn sat on his other side, surprising him.

Not caring who was watching, he grasped her hand and held on tight. Next play, Damon dropped back to pass the ball and was immediately wrapped up by Dwayne Carter, a New York cornerback.

Everything next happened in slow motion in Austin's brain. Damon was hit head on by Nick Markowski, a defensive end, and slammed to the ground, his head ramming against the turf.

They waited for him to get up. To move.

"Come on, man. Sit up," Austin said.

The announcers were discussing the fact that Damon remained on the ground, unconscious.

"Fuck!" Austin flew from his seat on a yell.

His mother screamed.

Quinn jumped up and grasped Austin's forearm, as they all watched in horror what unfolded on the big screen. They didn't need the announcers to tell them something awful had occurred or that they had to get to New York now.

Bri grabbed her mother's hand and Austin pulled his phone out of his pocket. Before he could call Ian Dare, his brother's team owner and the family member with a private jet, Austin's cell rang in his hand.

"Ian."

"I'm headed downstairs now," the other man said, out of breath as he obviously rushed to Damon's side.

"We need your plane," Austin said, he didn't ask.

"Done." For family, Ian would do anything. "The problem is it's in New York. I'm sending it back for you. Be ready in three hours." Ian disconnected the call.

Austin looked up to see his brother's face. Teammates swarmed him and as he suddenly opened his eyes. Trainers leaned over him and finally he was put on a stretcher and carried off the field.

Jesus. Austin's heart broke for his sibling. Despite being Damon's agent, Austin cared only about his brother's injury and pain and that he get the best treatment possible. The television was showing the play over and over.

"Amy?" Quinn's voice interrupted his thoughts as she spoke into her cell. "I need you to come over here and stay the night. Maybe a couple of nights. Austin's brother was hurt and we're going to New York." As Quinn spoke, she dropped one arm and grasped his hand in hers.

Quinn obviously wasn't letting Austin face Damon's injury alone, and he was grateful for her steady support.

"Who's coming to New York?" Austin asked the family. "Plane is in New York but Ian's sending it back here. We need to be ready in approximately three hours."

"I'm going," his mother said.

"Me," Bri added. "I'll take Mom to grab what she needs from home and we'll meet you back here?"

Austin nodded.

"We'll hold down the fort here." Paul was hugging Christine tight. "You guys go get ready. I'll have a car here for you to take you to the airport."

Realizing he still held Quinn's hand and his sister was watching them carefully, Austin deliberately didn't let go. She was his for as long as she'd stick by him and right now he needed her.

*　　*　　*

Along with his family and Quinn, Austin traveled on Ian Dare's private plane to New York. The trip was silent, everyone worried about Damon.

Quinn kept her hand inside his, giving him strength as he brooded, worried about his brother. He called Ian but all the other man could tell him was that they were running tests and when they had answers, he'd let them know.

They were an hour from landing when Austin's phone rang. "Ian. Talk to me."

"It's a severe concussion and it's not his first, as you know."

"Is he conscious?" Austin asked.

"Yes. But symptomatic."

Austin swallowed hard, knowing his mother and the rest of the family were listening. "We won't know anything about a return until he passes protocol." If he passed concussion protocol.

Something that would devastate his brother this early in a year that was supposed to lead to a new contract.

"Look—"

"No, I know. Let's focus on his health. Call me if you know more. We'll be there soon," Austin said, disconnecting the call. "Mom. It's a concussion. He's going to be okay."

His mom was sitting beside Bri and nodded, visibly relieved, but her tension would remain. She needed to see Damon for herself. They all did.

"Hey." Quinn spoke softly beside him. "What's going through your mind? Did Ian really say he's going to be okay or are you keeping the family calm until you know more?"

He turned and they were face-to-face, her lips inches from his. "Do you have any idea how much I appreciate you coming with me?"

Her smile warmed him inside. "I can't imagine how scared you all are feeling. I mean I'm worried and he's not my brother. I wouldn't leave you to deal with this on your own."

"That's twice now you've stood by me."

She grinned. "That makes you a lucky man," she said, brushing off what she'd done for him. "So how badly is this going to affect Damon's contract negotiations? I'm not trying to be cold, but I have a feeling that's what he's going to be focused on."

Austin smiled grimly because Damon's future was exactly what he'd been trying not to dwell on. "He has a solid history behind him with the Thunder. But I won't lie. A lot depends on his recuperation. What the doctors say. Whether it's safe for him to even return to play given that it's not his first or even third concussion. And even if he can return, it depends on whether Ian sees him as a liability." Ian might be family, but he had a team to run and a salary cap to keep in mind.

"Then it's a good thing Damon has the best agent in the business."

Her faith was humbling. "I'll do what I can for him."

"I know." She sighed. "When I was a year out of high school, my brother fell out of a tree house. I had to take him to the hospital because he was screaming in pain." She glanced out the window into the darkened sky.

"Where were your parents?" he asked.

"At work. They met us at the hospital, eventually. But I had to stay with him through x-rays, diagnosis, and getting his arm set." She turned to meet Austin's gaze. "I held his hand, not that he'd admit that to anyone," she said with a wry grin. "Guys are tough, you know."

"Yeah, I know. And I hope the doctors don't tell him he's had too many concussions to continue playing. He's had his share since he was a kid." He leaned his head against the back of the seat and turned toward her. "I hope your parents realize how lucky they were to have you holding down the fort on their behalf."

She shrugged. "It was expected. But don't get me wrong. Even if they'd been home, like you are now, I'd have been in the car with them going to the hospital to make sure he was okay."

"You just shouldn't have had to play parent or make decisions at nineteen."

"Yeah, well, that's the way it was. And it made me pretty self-sufficient. And a great executive assistant." She laughed, then said, "Which reminds me. I booked hotel rooms close to the hospital where they took Damon so everyone can come and go easily," she said.

He glanced at the woman who'd become so integral to his life. "Thank you. I didn't even think about where we'd stay."

She squeezed his hand. "You're welcome."

Not caring who was watching, he leaned forward and pressed his mouth to hers, rubbing his lips back and forth, tasting her since it was all he could do at the moment. She moaned softly into his mouth. "I need you, Quinn."

Before she could reply, an announcement came over the loudspeaker letting them know they would be landing soon.

As soon as they touched down, Austin heard Quinn call her niece and check on Jenny before he could pull out his phone and do the same.

For a woman who no longer wanted the responsibility of children and who knew Austin was now capable of the basics, she definitely continued to step up and make herself a part of both their lives. He didn't want to delude himself but her actions gave him a sliver of hope.

*   *   *

Hours later, Quinn sat in the hospital waiting area as the revolving door of people took turns seeing Damon. Despite the doctors and nurses limiting him to two visitors at a time, Damon was conscious and had remained so, and had agreed to see whoever had stayed to visit with him.

From family to coaches, teammates, and doctors, everyone got their five minutes. Ian took two. Quinn imagined that neither man wanted to talk much when the end result was so uncertain.

Austin went last, and when his turn came, he grabbed Quinn's hand, and before she could argue, not that she would in public, he pulled her through the doors and down the hall.

"Don't you want to see your brother alone?" she asked when it was just the two of them outside Damon's hospital room.

He turned to her, his indigo blue eyes somber. "Believe it or not, I could use the moral support. He's going to want answers I can't promise him.

She nodded in understanding. Austin was straddling the line between compassionate brother and honest agent. "Then let's do this."

Keeping her hand in his, Austin rapped on the door. "Incoming," he said and pushed the door open so he and Quinn could step through.

Damon lay against the pillows, his eyes glazed, looking pained.

Austin strode up to the foot of the bed. "Hey, buddy. If you wanted to sit out a preseason game, it would have been easier to just ask. You didn't need to get your ass kicked on the field." He joked but Quinn heard the hurt in his voice.

Damon winced, no doubt sensing his brother's empathy as well, and he let out a rumbling laugh. "Funny," he said, his voice rough. "Fuck. I didn't need this now." He glanced at Austin. "Ian could barely look at me."

"Doesn't mean he doesn't have faith in you. You're going to get through this."

Damon thinned his lips. "Thanks for the faith, man."

"I believe in you. I always will. Now let's deal with the immediate issues. How's the pain?"

Damon winced. "Not good." He glanced at Quinn. "Thanks for coming all the way to New York and keeping this guy company. Better be careful or you might become indispensable to him."

Austin glared but Quinn just ignored his teasing.

"You're welcome. I wanted to make sure you were okay, too," she said.

Damon leaned his head back against the pillows and yawned, the stress of the day obviously catching up with him. "If you weren't taken, I might appeal to your better nature and get you to stay here and look after me."

"I'm not taken," she said.

"Yeah? Then why hasn't he let go of your hand?" Damon chuckled and closed his eyes. "Night, love-birds."

Ignoring him, Austin walked out of the room.

Quinn didn't know what to say, either.

Chapter Nine

Austin's family had already left the hospital and headed to the hotel. His mom needed rest so she could get back to Damon early the next morning, and Bri had gone with her. Austin and Quinn took an Uber. On the way, he called Amy and checked on the baby, who had gone to sleep easily. He breathed out a sigh of relief.

Glancing at Quinn, he realized she'd tipped her head back and closed her eyes. Exhaustion was catching up to her, too. It really had been a long day, but seeing Damon had helped calm Austin down.

He let out a low groan and Quinn tilted her head, meeting his gaze. "Are you okay?"

"I didn't mean to wake you. I'm fine."

She shook her head. "I was just shutting my eyes for a few minutes.

The car pulled up to the curb in front of the hotel. They thanked the man and exited, grabbing their carry-on luggage from the trunk. At the front desk, they checked in to find their room was ready, and it didn't take long to head upstairs and settle in. Quinn had booked them one room with a king-sized bed and he was glad. He wanted nothing more than to lose himself inside her tonight.

While she closed herself in the bathroom to wash up, he stripped down to nothing but his boxer briefs and stood looking out the window at the city below. Glittering lights blinked up at him, cars honked, and ambulance sirens sounded. *The city that never sleeps* was an accurate description.

The bed had been turned down and mints left on the linen. He put the chocolate on the nightstand and sat down, leaning against the pillows, bracing his hands behind his head. Jesus, but today hadn't been anything like he'd planned.

No sooner had he closed his eyes than he heard Quinn step out of the bathroom. She wore one of his tee shirts, the large oversize cotton draping down to her knees.

"I packed fast," she said with a sheepish grin.

He scanned her tanned legs, imagined what was underneath the shirt, and his cock gave a jerk of approval. "I like you wearing my clothes." He held out an arm toward her, and she walked over, putting a knee on the mattress and pulling herself over him.

"Do you like me wearing *no* clothes?" She settled one leg on either side of him and met his gaze, her eyes darkening.

"Rhetorical question," he said, grabbing the hem of her shirt and pulling it over her head, revealing bare-naked skin and puckered nipples.

He pushed himself up and pulled one distended peak into his mouth, sucking hard until she responded, writhing on top of him and moaning his name. He lifted one hand and cupped her other breast, palming its weight and rubbing his thumb across her nipple. Playing with her breasts and watching her respond was arousing on its own, and his cock thickened beneath his boxer briefs. But he wasn't finished with her yet and gripped her waist in his hands, dragging his mouth down her rib cage, her stomach, until he couldn't dip his head any farther.

"These need to come off," she said, hooking her fingers into his waistband and wriggling the underwear down his thighs. She lifted herself so she could take them the rest of the way, and he kicked the material off and onto the floor. But before she could take control of any kind, he flipped her onto the mattress and held her down with one palm against her stomach.

"I need to taste you," he said and dipped his head between her thighs.

She smelled of musk and woman, and her scent aroused him. He licked, sucked, and teased her into oblivion, her body thrashing and her back arching up from the bed as he tormented her with his tongue. He swiped back and forth over her clit, the trembling in her limbs telling him she was close. He took her as high as he could and then nipped lightly with his tongue.

"Oh, God, Austin. So good. It feels so good." She pressed and rocked against his mouth, and he licked and laved her sex until the shaking slowed and she came down from her climax.

Then he slid off the bed and grabbed a condom from his carry-on and slid it on as he returned to the bed. Her hazy gaze met his, a warm smile on her face.

"You ready for another one, beautiful?"

"Let's see what you've got." She grinned and he bent down, kissing that smirk off her face.

He poised himself at her entrance and slid into her, her body easily adjusting to accommodate him as he filled her completely. He felt every ripple and warm squeeze of her inner walls around his cock and groaned.

And then he made her his, rocking into her, allowing his body to say the things he couldn't let himself speak. Instead of a hard pounding, he slid in and out slowly, his pubic bone grinding against her clit.

Soft moans escaped from the back of her throat.

Her arms locked around his neck.

Her lower body arched into him, holding on for dear life as she gripped him inside her.

"I want you to come again," he said, urging her to fall apart in his arms.

She shook her head. "I don't know if I can."

He slid a hand between them, slipping his finger over her clit. "I know you can." He pressed harder and made circles around and around until she was arching her back and clenching around him.

"Yes. I'm coming." She cried out, and as she spiraled, he began to thrust harder, deeper, until she pulled him over with her.

Afterwards, they lay wrapped up in each other in silence, Austin not wanting to bring up the subject of his mother's return to health, whether Damon would need her at home, or if she'd help out with Jenny. And of course, there was Amy, who had things well under control during the day and some evenings, buying Austin time until she went back to school in September.

There was no reason for Quinn to stay once they returned home, and he had a hunch she knew it. He also thought she didn't want to admit that a part of her wanted to remain with him. And Jenny? That he didn't know, but she checked on the baby as often if not more than Austin did.

Quinn sighed and snuggled back against him, and he wrapped his arms tighter around her. "Mmm," she muttered.

He agreed. She felt good. So good that, when his cock hardened, he adjusted his position and slid into her, finding her so wet for him she accepted him easily.

God, he loved her. He closed his eyes as her bare walls fluttered around him ... and he stilled. "I forgot a condom."

She stiffened but then he felt her relax. "It should be okay. Not the right time for me to get pregnant," she murmured.

Thank God. More complications were the last thing either one of them needed right now.

"You said it had been a long time for you?" she asked.

He nodded against her cheek. "I've been tested for insurance for the firm."

"And I had my yearly exam last month. We're fine. Now move," she said, arching against him.

Chuckling, he rocked into her, back and forth, over and over, until she stiffened, coming undone with his body curled around hers. One more thrust forward and he released himself inside her, recognizing he was in so fucking deep, and he didn't just mean literally.

* * *

The next morning, Quinn dressed to head back to the hospital. Austin sipped coffee in the main area of the hotel room, watching her intently, an intent look on his face. For the first time in a long time, she couldn't read him. She only knew he had something serious on his mind.

If it had anything to do with the way he'd slowly, reverently entered her last night, she was afraid to know. She'd never felt so cherished before, so cared for ... so loved. She had a lump in her throat she was afraid would never go away.

"I'm going to check on Jenny," she called out to Austin, needing a distraction.

Pulling out her phone, she dialed her cousin. "Hi, Ames."

"Hi! How is Mr. Prescott's brother?" Amy asked.

"In pain last night. We'll see when we get to the hospital this morning. What's going on there? Is Jenny okay?"

"She is. I think she's a little warm, so I'll take her temperature and give her baby Tylenol if she has fever. Don't worry. I can handle it."

"I know but if anything changes, and I mean anything, you call me." Quinn's heart picked up speed, worry consuming her. She knew babies got sick but this was *Jenny*.

"Okay. Oh! First thing this morning an overnight envelope came. I had to sign for them to leave it."

"Who is it from?" she asked so she could tell Austin.

"Michaelson Labs."

Quinn blew out a breath. The paternity results. "Thanks, Amy. I'll let you know when we'll be back. I should know something in a few hours."

"Bye." She disconnected the call and walked over to Austin, who had just put his coffee cup down.

"What's going on?"

Quinn swallowed hard. "Well, the paternity results were delivered this morning. Amy signed for them."

He closed his eyes and groaned, his fingers curling into fists.

"Hey." She pried open his fingers and slid her hand against his. "Every instinct I have says she's yours."

"And if she's not?" he asked, and she could swear his eyes were watery.

She treated him to a soft smile. "If not, you fight. Something tells me the star wide receiver and ace agent knows how to win."

He squeezed her hand tight. "I appreciate your faith."

"You've earned it. There's one more thing. Jenny has a slight fever."

His eyes opened wide. "We need to go home."

She loved his parental instincts. He was going to be a great father. "She might have a little cold. We'll see. Amy will call if anything changes and she knows how to give baby Tylenol. Let's go check on Damon and then make a decision."

He blew out a breath and sighed. "You're right. I need to see my brother. Then we can talk about leaving ... unless Jenny gets sicker."

"Sounds like a good plan."

He nodded. "Let's go." As he curled his hand around hers, they each grabbed a bag and he led her out of the hotel room.

*   *   *

Austin and Quinn returned to Miami along with Bri. His mother stayed in New York to help Damon travel back to Florida and get settled at home, which meant Ian's jet was getting quite the workout, flying back and forth to ferry the family where they needed to go.

Austin and Quinn arrived at his house to find Amy had just put the baby into bed for the night.

"How's she feeling?" he asked. "Temperature?"

"Normal. I'm sorry if I overreacted. I just thought she felt warm, and the first time I took her temp it was ninety-nine." Amy shuffled her feet, obviously worried.

"I'd rather you be proactive than say nothing. Besides, ninety-nine is something to watch. I'll keep an eye on her. Maybe bring her to the pediatrician tomorrow."

"I'll walk Amy out," Quinn said.

She'd been quiet on the way home, looking out the window more than she'd talked. He wondered what was going on in her head and almost didn't want to ask. But his gut told him they were coming to a point where she would have to make a choice and he wouldn't like the one she picked.

He sighed, left the luggage by the stairs, and walked into the kitchen. The envelope Amy had signed for waited for him on the counter, and he was drawn to it like a beacon. Inside was the answer he'd been waiting for, but in his heart, his decision had been made.

"Are you going to open it?" Quinn asked.

He leaned against the counter, staring at the white rectangular paper. "You know it doesn't matter, right? I mean, of course it matters, but the answer is going to make it easier or harder for me to fight and win."

She smiled and nodded but her heart wasn't in it, which meant his hurt knowing they were reaching the end.

"Open it," she murmured. "At least you'll know."

To his shock, his hand shook as he reached for the envelope. He picked it up and held it in his hand. A little over two weeks ago, he'd been a bachelor and content with his life. The thought of raising a baby had given him hives. Now the thought of turning Jenny over to anyone else made him physically ill.

He tore into the envelope and looked at the information on the page. He read through and his knees buckled. Quinn was there to grab him and wrap her arms around him as she peered around to see for herself.

"She's mine." His voice broke as the words came out. "Jenny's my baby."

"I'm so happy for you." She squeezed him tight, and he felt in her voice how much she meant the words.

Knowing he was choked up, he changed the subject somewhat. "Feel like going baby room shopping?"

She froze and he realized this was it. The moment he'd been dreading.

"I think I should go home," she said.

He stepped out of her embrace and turned to face her. "Why?" He'd already decided he wasn't going to make it easy for her to leave him. If she was going to walk away, she'd have to admit it was because of the baby.

Facing him, she drew a deep breath. Her eyes were rimmed red, and he knew this hurt her as much as it did him.

"You don't need me to care for Jenny anymore and we both know it. You've taken and passed the master class." She forced a grin but he didn't smile back.

"Anything I learned, it was from you. And I've seen you with the baby. Maybe you didn't go into this wanting kids, but can you deny how you feel about her now?" he asked, as if he could will her to admit her feelings.

"Of course I love her!" she blurted out.

His heart beat heavily in his chest. "Then stay."

She grasped on to the back of a kitchen chair, her fingers curling around the leather. "This was always a temporary arrangement."

Because they weren't a couple, and later he'd discovered she didn't want children of her own. But all that was before *them*. Before they'd come together in an explosion of passion, desire, and deep caring. For him it was love, but as he stared into her eyes, he remembered her telling him no one in her life cared about what she wanted. No one ever gave her the chance to make her own decisions. Which meant if he loved her, he needed to allow her that freedom.

He reached out, took her hand, and clasped it in his. "Jenny adores you. And I ... care about you, Quinn." He wouldn't admit that he loved her and use it as blackmail to make her stay. "And I know you care about me and Jenny."

She sniffed, as she nodded. "I do."

"Well, I believe we have a shot at something great, but you have to be ready. You have to want the same thing I do. And most importantly, it has to be your choice." He brushed his knuckles down her cheek. "So if you need to go, I understand."

*   *   *

A couple of hours later, Quinn found herself in her apartment. She'd only been gone a short time, but the entire place felt foreign to her, as if she hadn't slept there in months. With a sigh, she tried to remember her old routines but nothing came to her. Nothing but sadness as she recalled walking out of Austin's home, but she'd felt like she had no alternative.

For the last however many years, she'd bemoaned the fact that she'd raised her siblings and cousins, that she'd done her duty and didn't want kids. She'd ended her engagement to Daniel for that very reason. So faced with Austin, a man she cared for in a way she'd never felt for her ex-fiancé, and a baby she absolutely loved, she found herself looking at the life she'd claimed she did not want. And she'd run scared.

She was still scared.

Focusing on her apartment for now, she used Instacart to order food and, while she waited for the delivery, got to work cleaning out the old stuff in the fridge she'd forgotten about in her rush to go over to

Austin's and help him with whatever problem he'd deemed urgent.

That issue had turned out to be a baby. One who had captured her heart. Never mind the baby's father. What had started as a way to get him out of her system had quickly turned into so much more. He wasn't the playboy she'd pegged him for. Instead he was a man to admire. One to fall in love with. God, what had she done?

Her doorbell rang and she went to open it, checking through the peephole first, surprised to see not her food order but Evie on the other side. She opened the door and let her friend in. "What are you doing here?"

Evie, wearing a pair of baggy sweats, an oversized tee shirt and leather jacket, along with flip-flops, with a brown bag in hand, frowned. "You texted me that you were on your way home from Austin's for good, and you didn't expect your best friend to show up with pints of ice cream and an ear to hear why you left Mr. Wonderful and his adorable baby?"

Quinn blinked and tears fell from her eyes. "Come in here and give me the ice cream. You better have gotten one cookie dough for me."

"Of course I did. And a chocolate fudge brownie for me."

Before Quinn could close the door, the Instacart delivery woman arrived and Quinn accepted the bags.

"Thank you," she murmured.

"You're welcome. Have a nice night!" The woman walked off.

Quinn locked up behind her and headed to the kitchen, quickly putting the perishables away so she could return to Evie in the den and get started on her ice cream.

By the time she joined her friend, Evie had the television on and an old episode of *Friends* playing on the screen, which was much smaller than the huge display in Austin's family room. The thought made her sad, and she pulled the pint out of the brown paper bag, grabbing a spoon Evie had snagged from the kitchen.

Because Quinn's unpacking had taken a few minutes, the ice cream was a little soft, and she dug in, moaning at the delicious, creamy cookie taste.

She'd eaten three huge bites when Evie said, "Okay that's enough. Spill what happened tonight."

Caught mid-bite, Quinn met Evie's gaze, finished the ice cream, and sighed. "We got home from New York and Austin looked at the paternity test results. He's Jenny's father."

Remembering how relieved he'd been, how he'd nearly collapsed and she'd stepped up to hug him and hold him while he processed the news, her heart twisted in her chest.

"Is that good news or bad news?" Evie dug into

her chocolate and shoved a huge spoonful into her mouth.

Quinn managed to smile. "It's the best news. He'd already decided to keep Jenny regardless. This just gives him a legal leg to stand on once he finds the mother."

"It's crazy that she hasn't surfaced yet. Do you think she just wanted to get rid of her kid?" Evie asked.

Quinn shrugged. "Austin's gut is telling him she's going to want something in return for Jenny... eventually." They'd talked about that late one night.

Evie put her pint on a magazine on the cocktail table. "So why did you leave him then? Did he say he didn't need you anymore?"

Quinn shook her head. "He asked me to go shopping for baby furniture for Jenny's room." At the thought, her throat filled and her eyes welled up with tears.

Evie raised her arms in the air. "I'm fucking lost. You're going to have to spell it out for me, honey."

"Fine. We've been sleeping together, raising Jenny together, and creating a family together. In one short week, he demolished the walls I built, the feelings I had about not wanting children, and the preconceived notions I had about his willingness to settle down." After that rush of information, Quinn had to catch her breath.

"Whoa. So essentially you love him."

"I do." Quinn bobbed her head up and down, admitting it out loud for the first time. "He said he cares about me, and he thinks we can have something great if it's what I want, too." And God, she wanted that.

"Then why in God's name did you leave?" Evie asked.

Quinn had been asking herself that over and over. "Because I love him and I'm scared it won't work out. That he'll realize he just needed me for Jenny's sake. That his caring about me isn't the same as loving me." She rambled a list of excuses even she didn't believe.

Evie rolled her eyes. "For the love of God, for a smart woman, you're an idiot."

"What? Why? I have issues! Who doesn't? You're the one who thinks you intimidate every man you come in contact with."

She shrugged. "I do. I can kick their ass and they know it. But we're talking about you. And you walked away because you're scared. You're freaked out because the things you ran away from thanks to your family are now the same things you want. You think it's wrong to desire a family now. And you're scared to prove your mother right." Evie shrugged. "But guess what? It doesn't matter what your family thinks or wants. It only matters what *you* want."

Quinn nodded because Evie made sense. "I hate it when you're right."

Her friend grinned. "The ice cream is melting and I'll clean it in a second. But this is what you're going to do. You're going to take tonight and sleep in your apartment. You're going to see that the life here waiting for you isn't the one you want. And I'm going to sleep over because I'm opening a bottle of wine for us and I don't want to drive my car back home. Then, tomorrow, you're going to go to work and get your man."

Quinn smiled, her heart lighter than it had been since leaving Austin's earlier. She would have said it was impossible to change her mind about her life, but she had every right to do so. Even if the future freaked her out and might be uncertain.

Chapter Ten

Austin glanced at his watch again. Quinn had texted that she was running late this morning, and he wanted, no, he needed to see her.

After calling his family and spreading the news that Jenny was his baby, he'd spent the rest of the night pacing the floors and checking on the baby since it was his first time alone with her in the house. But she'd slept through, and he'd had no problem with her diaper or bottle in the morning.

Dressing her had been a little bit of a challenge, but he'd finally gotten her moving arms and legs into the right holes, and he'd handed her to Amy when she'd arrived on time. And though the morning had run like clockwork, he hadn't enjoyed it nearly as much without Quinn under the same roof.

He'd also received a call from the PI he'd hired to look into the woman he believed was Jenny's mother. Apparently she'd recently checked into a motel in downtown Miami using a credit card, which confirmed his suspicion that Nelle Jamieson was his baby's mother.

The PI was headed over to see if he could get answers from her, because Austin still believed she'd show up wanting money.

"Knock knock."

Austin glanced up to see his uncle in his office doorway. "Hey. Come on in."

"You looked a million miles away. Want to share what's going on?" Paul stepped inside. "I notice Quinn's not at her desk."

Austin smiled grimly. "Yes. She checked in. Said she'd be late."

Paul nodded. He chose a chair by the desk and sat down, crossing one foot over his leg. "How's your brother? I called this morning, but he's in a mood and not communicating much."

"Yeah. Damon didn't say much to me this morning, either."

Austin glanced at the professional photo of his brother with a football in his hand, uniform on, beside the one of Austin in the same pose, and prayed his brother returned to one hundred percent. Concussions were iffy suckers.

He flexed his fingers and groaned. "We'll deal with his business negotiations when it's time. Right now, Mom is going to accompany him home. We'll get him settled. It'll be okay."

This was Damon, his brother. And even if he were

only a client, Austin would do the same. He just wouldn't have as much of an emotional investment.

"And Quinn? Is she okay?" Paul drummed his fingers on the table beside him. "It's not like her to be late. You two have been coming to work together for the last week," he said pointedly.

Austin groaned, knowing his uncle was pushing for answers. "She moved out last night."

Paul raised his eyebrows. "Because you're suddenly ready to handle a baby, I presume."

"On the surface, yes. That's why."

"And if we dig deeper?" Paul asked.

Thinking about their conversation last night, Austin rubbed his palms against his eyes, which felt grainy from lack of sleep. "I asked her not to leave. I told her I care about her, that Jenny loves her, and I thought we had a shot at a future. But she had to want it, too."

Unfortunately she hadn't run into his arms. She'd run away.

"Let me get this straight. You told her you cared but you didn't tell her you love her?" Paul, the closest thing he had to a father ... hell, the man actually *was* his father, leaned close to the desk. "Why not?"

He could answer that easily. "Because all her life no one has given her a choice in what she wants. Her parents forced her to take care of her siblings and cousins. If they had their way, she'd be a nanny and not a fantastic executive assistant at a top sports agency. They don't know her and they don't respect what she wants. I do."

Paul shook his head as if he didn't understand or agree with Austin's decision. "Why would telling her you love her hurt anything?"

"Because if she feels the same way, she'd feel more obligated to give up her plans for her life. Which do not involve having kids. She needs to come to the choice to be with me and Jenny, to change her mind, free of undue influence." Even though it killed him not to tell her his feelings.

That he wanted to spend the rest of his life with her as his wife and Jenny's mother. He wanted to have more kids, kids who looked like Quinn.

He blew out a breath. "She has to want the same things I do. I can't force her to love me enough to change her mind about having children."

"You'll figure it out. You're two smart people. I have faith," Paul said, pushing himself up and rising from his seat.

"I'm so sorry I'm late!" Quinn rushed into the room, out of breath and not looking like his put-together Quinn. Her hair was pulled into a messy bun she usually reserved for home, her blouse was half tucked in, and she barely had makeup on her pretty face.

"It's fine. No meetings this morning," Austin said.

Paul greeted her and wished her a good morning before leaving them alone.

"Are you okay?" He didn't want to point out her shortcomings and sound like an ass. She always looked good to him, but this frazzled woman wasn't the female he'd grown used to seeing. Not even after dealing with a fussy baby first.

She blushed and met his gaze. "Evie came over last night. She opened a bottle of wine and one thing led to another... Well, I drank too much and overslept." She grinned sheepishly and adorably.

He wanted nothing more than to take her into his arms, hold her tight, and never let go. Instead, he managed a smile. "I'm sure you needed the girl time." He knew from Bri how important a woman's friends were during times of uncertainty and heartbreak.

Was her heart breaking like his was?

She walked over and took his hand. "Austin, listen..."

Her words were interrupted by the sound of his cell phone and he frowned. "Get it," she said.

He shook his head. "I want to hear what you have to say."

But before she could speak, her own cell began to buzz. She grabbed it from her bag. "It's Amy." She accepted the call. "Hi, Ames. What's up?"

As she listened, Quinn's eyes opened wide. "Okay, calm down and call your dad. Tell him to come over immediately. And set the alarm."

At her instructions, panic rushed through Austin since Amy was with Jenny. "What's wrong?"

Quinn met his gaze. "Someone is lurking outside the house. Amy was in the family room and saw a person in a hoodie walk by, then she ran to the front and saw them there, too."

"Jesus Christ. I'm going home." He started for the door but Quinn stopped him with a hand on his arm.

"Austin, Amy's dad is cop. He lives five minutes away. We'll go, but stay calm because my uncle Cal will be there first."

They ran to the car, not stopping to explain to anyone at the office where they were headed or why. Austin just needed to get home to his daughter. He floored it, not wanting to get pulled over but the desire to get home riding him hard.

They were about ten minutes from home when Quinn's cell rang. "It's Amy's cell."

"Put it on speaker," Austin said.

She tapped the screen twice. "Hello?"

"Quinn, it's Uncle Cal." In the background, it sounded like Amy was crying hysterically, and Austin's gut cramped in utter fear.

"What happened?" he asked.

"The doorbell rang. Amy was in a panic. She thought it was me, didn't check, and flung the door open. She had the baby in her arms."

"Son of a bitch," Austin muttered. "And?"

"A woman claiming to be Jenny's mother grabbed for the baby. Amy didn't want to fight her and hurt Jenny in the process, so when she yanked her, Amy let her go." Cal paused. "Shh. It'll be okay," he said to his crying daughter. "I'm back. The woman left you a note."

"What's it say?" Austin put his foot against the pedal harder, gripping the steering wheel tightly in his hands.

"There's a phone number. The note says call to exchange the baby for one hundred grand."

Austin slammed his hand against the wheel.

"I'm already tracing the number," Cal assured him. "We'll get her. As long as this woman thinks she's getting money, she's going to keep the baby safe."

Austin swallowed hard, doing his best to believe the other man, but it wasn't easy. "We'll be there soon."

As he drove, Quinn kept a calming hand on his leg, and he couldn't remember ever needing the support more.

* * *

Uncle Cal greeted Quinn and Austin at the door. He wasn't dressed for work, but he looked just as imposing as if he were in uniform.

Amy stood behind her dad, obviously afraid to face them, but she gathered her courage and peeked her head around her father's large body. "I'm so sorry, Mr. Prescott. I thought it was my dad at the door. I should have looked out, but I was scared and so relieved Dad was here." Her eyes were red from crying, her panic and fear obvious.

Quinn looked to Austin, afraid he'd turn his own panic and worry into anger at her niece, whose actions had been irresponsible but understandable.

He drew in a deep breath, obviously pulling himself together before he answered. "It's okay, Amy. I understand why you opened the door. Let's just focus on getting Jenny back. I don't blame you for what happened."

Relief washed over Amy's face, and Quinn had never been so grateful to anyone as she was to Austin for how gently he'd handled her niece.

Austin glanced at Cal. "What now?"

Cal's cell pinged and he glanced at the screen. "Now we go to the motel and get your baby back. The address is right here." He flashed the screen to Austin.

"That's the motel my PI checked out this morning. She wasn't there."

"I need proof the baby is yours before I can put this in motion," Cal said. "Otherwise I can't give the baby back to you. I'll have to turn her over to social services. Because we're definitely taking the mother in for extortion, kidnapping, child abandonment, and anything else we can nail her with." He spoke with the determination of a man used to getting things done.

"The paternity test is on the kitchen counter," Austin said.

"Grab it and I'll call for backup."

Quinn breathed yet another sigh of relief that the test had come back and Austin was Jenny's dad. She couldn't imagine him having to hand her over to the police or a civil servant. It would have broken him.

She grasped on to Austin's hand. "I'm coming with you."

"You're damn right you are." He pulled her along with him to get the paper and then to meet up with Cal in the front hall.

"Amy, you're staying here. Call your mom to come get you or sit with you, but I don't want you driving when you're this upset," Cal instructed his daughter.

"Okay, Dad. Good luck." She closed the door and they heard the sound of the lock click.

"You two are staying in the car," Cal said as they walked to his vehicle. "I'm meeting up with uniformed officers in the lot. We'll go in and get the baby." He pressed his key fob and unlocked the door.

Instead of getting into the front passenger side, Austin nudged Quinn into the back seat along with him, and Cal nodded, seeming to understand.

"I want to be there when you confront her, and I want to be the one she hands my daughter to," Austin said, clenching his fists.

Cal started up the car. "And I can't risk having a civilian get hurt. So you're going to stay in the back or you're not coming. I promise to bring your daughter back to you immediately, and you can talk to the mother back at the police station."

Austin grumbled his agreement, and Quinn snuggled close to his side, wanting to give him comfort as much as she needed it herself.

Ten minutes later, they'd pulled up to the motel and parked in the far corner. Cal was in an unmarked car and he left them in the back while he headed inside to find out the woman's room number. If she hadn't checked in under her real name, he had Austin's description and a photograph on file from the DMV that had been sent to him on his phone.

With Quinn's heart pounding in her chest, she and Austin sat in silence, each lost in their own thoughts and fear.

Backup arrived, sirens off, and they conferred with Cal, who'd returned with the room number, then Cal stomped over to the car and leaned inside. "I'm warning you two, stay put." He shook his finger at them. "We've got this."

"Fine." Austin was pissed, his body vibrating in anger, but even he wasn't going to argue with armed cops.

Quinn was petrified for Jenny but she believed in her uncle and she turned to Austin. "Hey."

She waited until he looked at her and really focused. "If Cal says Jenny is safe as long as Jenny's mother thinks you're delivering money, I believe him. He's been a cop since he was nineteen. You can trust him to bring her back to you," she said softly.

"I want to be the one knocking on that door. Grabbing my baby. Facing the bitch who thought leaving her alone on my doorstep was a good idea. Trying to extort money from me." His voice rose in anger as he spoke.

She held on to his hand, his touch warm and rough in hers. "I know. But sometimes you have to let the professionals do their jobs."

A muscle ticked in his jaw, and she ached to lean forward and kiss him, calm him, but she'd given up that right last night.

"You do realize when this is over we're going to talk?" he asked as if reading her mind.

Her heart squeezed at the knowledge but she held

on to hope. "I know." As she looked into the eyes of the man she loved, she wondered how she'd ever walked out of his house last night. How she'd let a decision to not have kids, one she'd made at eighteen years old, rule her life when her feelings for Austin were so strong.

When she looked back on her past relationships or almost-relationships, she could see how things played out. Last night, alone in her bed, she'd realized she'd let Daniel go because she hadn't wanted to have *his* baby. She hadn't wanted to marry *him*.

And in high school, she'd missed so many activities with friends and lost a boy she'd wanted to date because she'd had to be caregiver to her siblings and cousins. As a result, she let herself walk out on the man she loved because she was afraid to admit she wanted the very thing she'd discounted.

What a mess. She needed to own her feelings, admit them out loud, and hope Austin still wanted to try with her. That leaving him hadn't shattered his trust in her.

But first came getting Jenny back. Nothing mattered more than that.

*   *   *

Time ticked by slowly, and Austin felt as if he were coming out of his skin waiting for the police to return.

He couldn't see the motel room from his position in the car, which was probably for the best. Nothing would stop him from getting his kid if he had a visual on her, that much he knew.

Beside him, Quinn was solid. A rock. Holding on to him and keeping him calm. Talking to him about her uncle and telling him stories about successful situations he'd found himself in and repeated at family dinners. Austin needed to hear those things, and she knew just what to say.

Finally, he saw Cal walking his way with a baby in his arms. He vaguely registered the uniformed officers behind him with a familiar-looking woman being led to a police cruiser.

He didn't remember opening the door or getting out or running across the lot. He didn't even recall grabbing Jenny and taking her from Cal. He just knew that suddenly he was on his knees on the asphalt, his baby in his arms, the sweet smell of her shampoo filling his senses and tears falling from his eyes. And he didn't even give a shit that he was crying in public.

"What happened?" Quinn asked her uncle.

"Too damned easy." He spread his hands wide. "She opened the door expecting it to be Austin." He shook his head. "She started crying about needing the money and being unable to support a baby and keep her job as a flight attendant."

"So why didn't she just come to me and tell me she was having my baby?" Austin asked, now standing up, holding Jenny close.

Cal sighed. "Because she has mental health issues she tried to hide from the airline, but they found out and fired her. She apparently thought it would be better to extort a lump sum from you and walk away ... planning to return whenever she needed cash by threatening to file for custody." Cal pointed to his temple and swirled his finger in the age-old gesture of *crazy*.

"I'm making her sign away parental rights." Austin was getting his lawyer on that immediately.

"I don't think you'll have much of a problem even if you did have to end up in court to get it done. She can't take care of herself let alone an infant." Cal glanced at Quinn, who was watching Austin with the most loving smile on her face.

He pressed a kiss to the baby's soft head. "Nobody's taking you from me." But he held the baby out for Quinn.

Her eyes welled as she accepted the infant and cuddled her close. "Hey, little girl. You gave us quite a scare. We're going to teach you not to go anywhere with strangers," she said, wrapping her arms tighter around Jenny, dipping her head, and taking a moment to just breathe.

Austin caught the word *we*. *We're* going to teach you. Maybe a night away from them had taught her what she really wanted out of life. He could only hope.

Cal cleared his throat. "We'll need a statement from Amy, me, and of course you," he said to Austin. "But it can wait until morning. Take the baby home and get some sleep. If you have the original note she left with the baby, bring that with you to the station."

Austin nodded. "I want a word with her." He tipped his head toward the squad car holding Nelle Jamieson.

"Make it quick," Cal said.

Austin glanced at Quinn.

"I've got her. Go ahead."

Drawing a deep breath, Austin walked with Cal to the open back door of the squad car and stared at the woman he remembered from the bar in Chicago. Back then she'd been in a tight dress, her hair had been in waves around her shoulders, and her makeup perfect. Now? She looked like she'd been through a rough patch. Her hair was a tousled mess, her makeup smudged beneath her eyes, and her expression was defeated.

"Why?" Austin braced a hand on the top of the car and glared down, wanting to hear the excuse from her. "Why not come to me and just tell me you were pregnant?"

"You wouldn't have believed me. Besides, I needed you to want her. To keep her safe. Then you'd get attached and give me the money I needed." She struggled against the cuffs holding her hands behind her back.

"So you left an infant alone on my doorstep in the dark? At night?" he asked, his voice rising.

Nelle dipped her head but she looked up at him, embarrassed, at least. "I hung around until you came home. I knew you took her inside," she said defensively.

"Not good enough. Look, lady, you are never going to see *my* baby again. You'll be getting an agreement to dissolve all parental rights from my lawyer. I expect you to sign it."

"What's in it for me?" she had the nerve to ask.

"Jail time for anything the cops can come up with." He slammed his hand on the top of the car and walked away, heading back to where Quinn was waiting with Jenny.

Cal joined him and Austin faced Quinn's uncle. "I don't know how to thank you."

"I'd say I was just doing my job but we both know this was more." He smiled then. "Thank you for being so good to my daughter. You could have gone off on her and I'd have understood." He ran a hand over his face.

"Let's just focus on the fact that we got Jenny back and it ended well. Amy's a good kid. I'm happy to have her continue to work for me. These were ... extenuating circumstances," Austin said.

"And she learned a big lesson." Cal's smile was grim. "I'll drop you two off at Austin's. Okay?"

Quinn nodded.

"Thanks again, Cal. For everything."

*   *   *

Since they didn't have a car seat, Austin held on to Jenny during the short ride home. Quinn sat in the far corner near the car door, watching them, her heart in her throat. The love Austin had for Jenny was genuine, real, and ran deep already. She felt the same way. Although her uncle had reassured them they'd get the baby back safely, deep down, she'd known anything could go wrong. Thank God it hadn't. Quinn was only now beginning to breathe normally again.

Cal dropped them off in the driveway, and Quinn accompanied Austin into his house, waiting downstairs while he took Jenny up to her crib. The baby had fallen asleep in his arms, and Quinn assumed she'd transfer easily.

She strode around the house, waiting so they could talk. From the hallway with the modern bold paintings to the kitchen with the array of bottles and nipples spread all over to the family room with the baby swing, the entire house felt like home. *Her* home. Much more than the apartment she'd returned to last night.

"Hey." Austin joined her in the family room.

"Hi. Did she go down okay?" Quinn asked about Jenny.

He nodded. "She's sleeping like a baby." He grinned at his poor joke. "Honestly she's going to bounce back from this much quicker than I will." He walked to the sliding glass door and looked out at the pool area. "Thank God Nelle just handed over the baby to Cal. This could have gone down so much worse."

Quinn walked up behind him and wrapped her arms around his waist, his warm, masculine scent a balm to her still-shaking insides. "But it didn't. You have your little girl back."

He spun suddenly, switching their positions so her back was against the cool pane of glass, his arms braced on either side of her head. "Do *I* have my girl back? Or do we have our little girl back?" he asked, his dark indigo eyes boring into hers.

She swallowed hard, understanding that this was the defining moment in her life. What she said now could change everything. "I'm sorry I left last night. I hurt you and that wasn't my intention."

"I know."

She swallowed hard. "But I needed a night to catch my breath and to come to terms with the fact that what I thought I wanted had changed. And that it was okay for me to do a one-eighty and it didn't make me a hypocrite."

She blinked and tears fell from her eyes. He reached out and swiped a droplet with his finger. His expression was soft as he watched her and allowed her to explain.

"I also had to accept that it would be okay to end up with what my mother thought was best for me all along." She smiled wryly. "But most importantly I realized that having a family doesn't mean I have to give up everything else in my life. It's not like you'd fire me as your assistant." She batted her eyelashes at him. "Would you?"

He let out a laugh. "Of course not. I can't function without you at work or at home."

She sobered then. "So you understand? Why I needed last night? What I said, it makes sense to you?"

"Oddly? Yes, it does. Because I know you. And I know that you haven't been given many choices in your life when it came to babies. And kids. And those are huge responsibilities. So you needing time was normal. Human even."

God, she didn't deserve this man. This good, kind,

giving, understanding man.

"That's why I didn't tell you how I really feel about you last night," he said. "Because I didn't want to pressure you. You needed to make your own choice about whether you wanted a ready-made family."

"I do." She cupped his cheeks in her hands and stared into the face she loved. "I love you, Austin."

"And I love you. I wish I'd told you last night, but I'm glad you had the time to come to me on your own. I want you free and clear. I want us. I want a family with you."

Her lips lifted in a happy smile. "I want that, too."

"But I need to be clear. When I say family, I mean kids with you, too. A little boy or girl with dark hair and green eyes—"

"Those Dare eyes are pretty dominant," she said, laughing.

He grinned. "Okay, I'll take any color eyes. I just want more kids with you. Jenny is mine and she's yours, Quinn. We're a family."

She nodded. "We are."

"But we're us, too. You and me. And I love you. Not the built-in babysitter you once thought you were. Not the nanny you might have been. There's no one else for me, Quinnlyn Stone."

"There's no other man for me, Austin Prescott."

"Then let's seal the deal. Strip for me, Quinn."

A few minutes later, her back was against the glass door, her legs around his waist, and he thrust deep inside her, joining them in the most elemental way possible. He wasn't wearing a condom. And she didn't care at all.

Epilogue

A few weeks later, Austin woke up wrapped around a naked Quinn to the sound of his phone ringing. He felt for his cell on the nightstand and answered without looking at the caller, but he'd caught the time and it was eight a.m. Apparently they were running late this morning, but he and Quinn both needed sleep, and Jenny seemed more than willing to oblige. She'd only woken once last night.

He put the phone to his ear. "Yeah."

"Austin, it's Damon."

He immediately caught the edge of panic in his brother's voice. "What's wrong?" He pushed himself to a sitting position in bed.

Quinn woke up and sat up beside him, a worried expression on her face.

"I took a random drug test and apparently I tested positive for PEDs." Performance-enhancing drugs banned by the NFL.

"Son of a bitch."

"I didn't fucking take them, Austin. Not even supplements. Nothing. I swear."

Austin shook his head. "No need to swear to me, little brother. I believe you. Now listen to me. Call Bri. Other than that, talk to no one. Not the press, not even Ian again. I'll be right over."

He disconnected the call and turned to Quinn. "Damon tested positive for PEDs. There's no fucking way my brother cheated. I don't know what happened but we have to clear his name."

Quinn blinked at him and he could see her smart brain already working. "Let me call Evie."

He narrowed his gaze, trying not to look at her bare breasts as she sat beside him in bed. Grinning, she pulled up the covers. "Yes, Evie. Pay attention. She's a PI. And I promise you she's the best there is. I don't know what you'll need but my gut tells me she can help."

He nodded. "Okay, but let's meet with Damon and Bri first. I need us all to be on the same page before we bring in an outsider."

His phone rang again. He looked at the screen and muttered a curse. "It's Ian." Austin took the call. "Hello?"

"I assume you've heard the news? What the fuck, Austin?" Ian sounded like one pissed-off NFL team owner.

"Am I talking to my cousin or Damon's boss?"

Quinn curled her hands around his bicep in support.

"For the moment? Your cousin."

Austin blew out a relieved breath. Ian was going to be reasonable, at least for now. "He didn't take shit, Ian. I promise you that." Austin would trust his brother and swear on his own life.

"Then prove it," Ian said and disconnected the call.

With a groan, Austin laid his head back against the pillow. "Son of a bitch. When the press gets ahold of this…" He didn't need to continue. He knew Quinn understood the ramifications.

"What's next?" she asked.

"Family meeting."

She met his gaze, an uncertain look in her eyes, and he could read the question in her expression: Should she come? Was she welcome? Or were they closing ranks tight?

He held out a hand and she placed her palm against his. "Welcome to the Prescott family, Quinn." He thought about the situation, all the parties involved, and managed a grin. "Welcome to the Prescott-Dare family," he amended.

She threw her arms around him, and he pulled her on top of him, their bare bodies molding together. Unfortunately they had no time for fun.

As for her place in this family? An engagement

ring was next on his list of things to do after he settled his brother down. They might only have been together for a week, but he and Quinn had had a year of getting to know each other behind them.

She was his.

And he belonged to her.

Now and forever.

Don't miss the next DARE NATION series book
DARE TO TEMPT with Damon Prescott and
Evie Wolfe.

DARE TO TEMPT

He's a smooth talking jock.
An ace quarterback.
And suddenly screwed.

Damon Prescott had it all. Star quarterback. Money.
Fame. Now? He's being accused of taking performance enhancing drugs and banned from the sport
and team he loves.

Determined to prove he's innocent, he hires tough as
nails private investigator, Evie Wolfe. She's able to
bring a man to his knees with a glare, yet sensual in
ways that take him off guard—and she's everything
Damon didn't know he needed.

Evie's used to men dismissing her, especially playboys
like Damon Prescott so she's not buying the sexual
lines he's trying to sell. She's with him to do a job,
nothing more. But you know what they say about the
best laid plans? Sometimes you end up between the
sheets with an arrogant football player anyway.

But when the case is over, can Damon convince Evie

she's the only woman for him or will she leave him tied up in love?

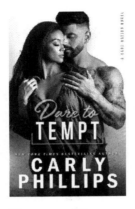

Dare to Tempt
Dare Nation Novel #2

Chapter One

Damon Prescott's life had gone from golden to shit in an instant. Or rather in one violent football play gone wrong. He refused to watch the reviews of his injury. The slam of his head against the turf and the shattering pain before he blacked out were vivid enough in his mind.

Another concussion should have been the worst of his problems. Instead he'd also tested positive for performance enhancing drugs and when the hospital had turned his records over to the team doctors, which he'd signed off on because what did he have to hide, he'd been suspended immediately. As if he'd touch the stuff. No unknown supplements went into his body. Period. So how the fuck had he tested positive not just once but on a second check, as well?

A knock sounded at his door and he pushed himself up from his couch, his head still pounding a week later. Even his ears continued to ring. He walked slowly to the front entrance, opened up and let his family into his home. It was the second meeting since the results had come back.

The people entering his house weren't just family, they were his team. Dare Nation, a sports management firm, his brother, Austin, owned along with their Uncle Paul Dare.

Austin, his oldest sibling and his agent, strode in first, his executive assistant and girlfriend, Quinn Stone by his side. Austin patted him on the back. Quinn smiled and murmured her apologies for what was going on.

Next came Bri, his sister and publicist. "Don't worry, I've got you covered," she promised him, pulling him into a hug.

He'd deliberately kept this gathering tight. He didn't want his mother here. She was already upset by the situation and his injury. His brother, Jaxon, was on the road playing baseball and Braden was abroad with Doctors without Borders. And Paul was at the office, fending off the press and holding down the fort there.

But they did need a plan. First of all, the seasons started in two weeks and he didn't want to miss being allowed on the field for the first four games due to a suspension. He was appealing the suspension and should hear soon what the verdict was. He hadn't cheated, dammit.

Austin cleared his throat. "Let me start by saying everyone in this room knows you didn't cheat. But we also know the likelihood of winning on appeal in this zero tolerance era and it's not good."

Damon clenched his fists at his sides. "I did not take a banned substance."

His brother stared at him, his expression somber. "Players are responsible for what is in their bodies and a positive test will not be excused because a player was unaware he was taking a prohibitive substance." He repeated the words from the players' collective bargaining agreement.

Words Damon already knew by heart.

"Golden Tate was taking fertility treatments he didn't know contained prohibited substances," Austin continued. "And if that doesn't tug on the committee's heartstrings I don't know what will."

"Tate self-reported before he tested positive and they still didn't cut him any slack," Bri said.

Despite the fact that Damon heard his siblings, he

refused to give up without a fight and believing in himself was priority one. "I still say we go forward as if we'll win. We thought we'd hear by now. Maybe it's a good sign they're taking their time."

His brother and sister glanced at each other and nodded.

"We figured you'd say as much," Bri said. "So. I've got an idea. Well, thanks to Quinn, I have an idea."

Damon grinned. "You're the family fixer. Of course you do." But he rubbed his chest, which grew tight any time he let himself think about the mess he was in.

Without admitting it to his siblings, even he knew that the only out given on appeal was when the testing had been compromised. He couldn't prove his had. But he refused to give up until forced to.

It was a contract year for fuck's sake. The positive test gave Ian Dare, his team owner, every reason not to offer him the deal he deserved as the up and coming star quarterback of the Miami Thunder.

"You've spoken to Ray Benson's P.I.?" Damon asked of the lawyer both Dare Nation and Austin himself used when his baby girl had been left on his doorstep almost two weeks ago.

So much had changed in such a short time.

Bri shook her head. "Nope. I have someone better. A licensed PI who I trust." She clasped her hand behind her back and rocked on her heels, grinning in a way Damon didn't trust.

His gut churned and he glanced at Austin. "You wouldn't let her fuck me over, right?"

Austin rolled his eyes. "We're all on your side. Though I will say Bri's plan is a little ... unorthodox."

Before either could elaborate, the doorbell rang. Damon raised his eyebrows. "Who is that?"

"I've got it," Bri said and rushed to the front of the house to let the unknown visitor in.

Damon waited and seconds later, Bri strode back into the room with his biggest nightmare by her side. Evie Wolfe, Quinn's best friend, a *licensed PI*, and a woman Damon hadn't been able to get out of his head since the day they'd met, walked in.

Evie wasn't anything like the type of female he was used to. No red-soled stilettos or designer handbags for her. She wore a pair of ripped jeans and scuffed leather boots that fit her like a glove. His gaze traveled upward to a tight white tee-shirt that dipped low and showed off her cleavage, topped off by a light weight black leather jacket she rarely removed. Even on a hot summer day. And damned if it wasn't fucking sexy.

Added to her appeal, her long dark hair hung loose to her waist and she eyed him with an amused grin. "Hi, Damon."

"Evie."

They'd met a few times over the last year that her best friend had worked at Dare Nation and they'd definitely gotten under each other's skin. He didn't know what it was about her but he was more comfortable across the room and not close enough to smell her musky perfume.

"Well, who wants to hear the plan?" Bri asked.

He folded his hands across his chest and glared at his sister who was enjoying her moment way too much. "Go on."

"You tested positive for PED's and you think you were set up," Evie said.

"I know I was set up," he said through clenched teeth.

Evie nodded. "And you need to know who did it, how, and why."

"Which is why I need a private investigator."

She grinned. "One who can stay by your side and get into places a regular P.I. can't. Places a girlfriend can go." She sidled up to him, rubbing her leather-clad arm against his bare one and damned if his body didn't respond, his cock perking up.

Then her words registered. "Oh hell no." He didn't *date* women, real or pretend.

He fucked them and sent them on their way. And he didn't think he had a shot in hell of anyone believing he was together with Evie and her leather clad body. Despite what his dick wanted, something he'd yet to understand.

"Damon, think about it. You need someone who can evaluate the people in your life."

"In case you forgot, the suspension means I can't do much with anyone on the team," he reminded her.

"Yes but they can't stop you from *running into some-one* in a public place." She put quotation marks around the words she'd emphasized. "So if there's anyone you want to meet, he can subtly arrange it. This is exactly what we wanted," Bri said with excitement in her voice. "And most importantly, I trust her."

Evie checked him with her hip. "Come on. How can it hurt? Unless you're afraid of me?"

He gritted his teeth. "Of course I'm not afraid of you. I just don't think we're ... compatible or that it'll look real," he said, scanning from her scuffed boots to her wind blown hair, ignoring the fact that he thought she was gorgeous in an understated and quite unique way.

She stepped in front of him and braced her hands on her hips. A flush of red stained her cheeks.

"Embarrassed to be seen with me?" she asked, telling him he'd been right. He'd hit a nerve. "Because I promise you I can dress up and play a role as well as any one of those football females you and your buddies hang out with," she assured him.

From across the room, Austin glared. Because Evie was Quinn's best friend? Or because Damon was being stubborn about a plan Austin had faith in? Probably a combination of both.

"Tell you what," Austin said. "Let's go to Allstars tonight and test the theory of you two as a couple."

Damon considered the idea. The upscale bar would have enough people there to see them together and for them to get a feel for whether people familiar with Damon bought the concept of Evie as his girlfriend. He could handle testing things out. "Fine."

"Don't sound so thrilled." Evie scowled at him. "I'm going home. Apparently it's going to take me a long time to pull myself together for his highness over here." She jerked a thumb his way, making Damon feel like shit.

He hadn't meant to insult her, just explain why he didn't believe this plan would work.

"I'm going with you." Quinn picked up her purse, shot a nasty look at Damon, and followed her best friend out, leaving Damon with his siblings. And he damn well knew if Quinn was pissed at him, so was Austin.

"Well that went well," he said aloud.

"Because you're an asshole," Bri said. "Evie didn't deserve to be insulted considering she was willing to help you."

Damon stiffened his shoulders. "I didn't think I was offending her. Just being honest."

"You as much as told her people wouldn't think she was your type, Bro." Austin leaned against the wall unit in the family room.

"Actually the way he looked her over all but insinuated she wasn't feminine enough," Bri said.

He winced.

"Okay look, you're not in a position to fight this," Bri reminded him. "A regular PI can't talk to the people around you. She can. So suck it up and make nice."

"I'll see you tonight. I'll text you the time. Want us to pick you up because you can't drive?"

"I'll take a driver." He had a feeling Quinn would lay into him if they were alone. And the three of them might show up with Evie.

Damon needed time to prepare himself for the act of a life time.

"I'll see you tonight. I expect you to be on your best behavior."

Damon frowned. "Are you speaking as my brother or my agent?"

"Both." Austin stood up straight and started for the door. "And you could start with an apology to Evie."

Bri smirked, liking when someone else was getting

called on the carpet. "Hang in there, Damon. You can trust Evie to get the job done." She paused. "As long as you're not an asshole to her, that is."

Ignoring her comment, he let his family out and leaned against the door with a groan. He was exhausted and needed to lay down if he was going to go out for an hour or so tonight. At least Allstars was quiet, known for letting athletes and famous people mingle in peace without groupies begging for autographs or signed boobs.

Speaking of boobs, he wondered how much cleavage Evie would show tonight. Jesus, he was an asshole. Blaming the concussion, he headed upstairs to take a nap before his performance later tonight.

*   *   *

"Stupid jackass," Evie muttered as she yanked a hairbrush through her long hair. It was knotted from the ride in her convertible and she stood in front of the mirror on the wall in her bedroom, trying to get the tangles out.

Brainless no-good, dark-haired, sexy, tattooed, bastard with full lips, tanned skin and indigo blue eyes. She blew out a puff of air and ignored the tingling of her skin and the rush of arousal that always accompanied her thinking about Damon Prescott.

Quinn sat cross-legged on the bed and Evie could

see her in the reflection. "He didn't mean to be a jackass. He's in pain and he's frustrated."

Evie turned to her best friend. "Are you standing up for him?"

"No." She held up her hands, making it clear whose side she was on. "I just don't want you to lose out on a good job. Not to mention we need you. Ignore Damon's attitude. I'm sure Austin straightened him out when we left."

"Fine but if he says anything rude tonight he's getting a stiletto in his foot."

Quinn grinned, a real smile. Since falling in love with Austin and taking on the role of mom to the baby girl he'd found on his doorstep, she was lighter and happier than she'd ever been.

"Or we could sic all four of your brothers on him. That could be fun. If he wasn't injured, that is."

Evie rolled her eyes. "Now that you're attached to the family you're no fun," Evie said. "You're too nice."

"What are you going to wear tonight?" Quinn ignored her comment, slid off the bed and headed to her closet to look through her dresses.

Evie narrowed her gaze, remembering how that handsome jerk had looked her over and found her lacking. Damon Prescott pushed all her wrong buttons. From the day she'd been introduced to him at a party for Paul Dare that Quinn had convinced her to attend, he'd treated her like an annoyance. So she couldn't deny the idea of dressing up and seeing his jaw drop at the sight of her held a lot of appeal.

"This." She joined Quinn by her walk-in and reached for the black one-armed dress that draped her body and hit mid-thigh.

"Oooh pretty. Reminds me of my red gown and Austin nearly ripped that right off me." She grinned at an obvious memory Evie didn't want to know about.

"Keep the dirty details to yourself."

"You know … you don't need to cover your arm. The scar has healed and—"

"We don't discuss it, remember?" Evie laid the dress out on the bed and smoothed her hand over the soft fabric.

"*You* don't discuss it. I do because the past doesn't define who you are, no matter what you think." Quinn put her hands on her hips and faced Evie. "Now I'd love to lend you a gold dress that would look gorgeous with your skin tone. It drapes down the back and both arms are bare."

Evie shook her head. "A married woman hired me to catch her husband cheating and it turned out he was my fiancé. A man I hadn't pegged as dangerous and I should have. I'd say that shows a decided lack in judgment on my part when I prided myself on being a smart chick."

Quinn gave her a sympathetic look. "You're still a smart chick. John was a slick bastard. He conned his wife as well as you and she's an investment banker. I don't think she's stupid. Do you? What about the other women who've been duped by pathetic men? Who's at fault?"

"I hear you but it isn't the same thing. I need my instincts and if I can't trust those, then I have issues I need to work through. And *this* is a reminder of my mistakes." She held out her arm with the angry red scar running along her forearm.

"I don't want it exposed so I can see it every day or be asked about it and have to explain the knife wound." Because John, once cornered, had come out fighting and he hadn't hesitated to cut her to get away.

Tears formed in Quinn's eyes and she pulled Evie into a hug, something she still wasn't used to, even though Quinn had always been a hugger. Her brothers were more the shoulder slapping types but they always had her back. Always. And they'd have gone after John if she hadn't insisted she didn't want them to end up behind bars.

"Okay fine. I'm not going to give up trying to convince you that you're the strong, kickass woman you always were but tonight wear that dress. When he gets a look at you, Damon is going to swallow his tongue.

Now let's see the shoes."

A couple of hours later, Quinn had gone home to see Austin and Jenny, the adorable little baby, and change for tonight.

Evie stood in front of the mirror once more and she didn't recognize herself. It had been a long time since she'd dressed up for any reason or gone all out for any occasion.

She'd put self-tanner on her legs, arms, chest and face, because she never had the time to relax and lay in the sun. Her face was completely made up, including wearing false eyelashes, her lips were plump, and her gorgeous brown eyes wide.

The dress accentuated her curves while the designer red-soled heels hurt her damned feet. Though she had to admit she liked the Chanel purse she owned for times when she had to look a certain way. And tonight? She appeared every inch the pro football player's girlfriend. Damon Prescott wasn't going to know what hit him.

*   *   *

Given his concussion, Damon couldn't drink alcohol. It was hard enough to hold up his head but he understood the need to be out tonight. If he wanted to discover who had set him up, he needed to put a plan in motion and testing Evie and their chemistry was a start.

So he sat at a table at Allstars with Austin, Quinn, Bri and her best friend, Charlotte. Surrounding them were other guys from his team, Devon White, his running back and James Slater, his wide receiver. Marnie, the cocktail waitresses, an auburn-haired, stunning woman, knew them all by name and took drink orders, fawning over Damon and his injury.

Beside him, Austin shifted in his seat so many times Damon grew agitated. "Bro, what the fuck? You're annoying as hell." Damon elbowed Austin in the arm.

Quinn grinned. "Your brother took Marnie home the night he found Jenny on his doorstep."

Damon tipped his neck back and burst out laughing, immediately regretting the motion when his head began to pound. Dammit these symptoms were lasting a long time. "I have to admit that was worth the pain."

Austin shot him a dirty look but Quinn merely cuddled up closer to Austin and continued to smile.

"At least you're not the jealous type," Damon said, to the pretty woman with dark hair and green eyes, who seemed custom made for Austin.

Not that they hadn't had their issues. Between Quinn not wanting kids, Austin being handed a baby by another woman, and her being his brother's assistant, they'd overcome a lot in a short time.

"That's only because Marnie's keeping her distance from your brother." Quinn's gaze traveled across the room to where Marnie filled drinks by the bar.

"And that's because you're wrapped around me, staking your claim. Besides, I only have eyes for you." Austin leaned over and pressed a kiss against her lips.

"You two are making me want to barf." Bri picked up her bottle of Blue Moon and took a long sip.

Charlotte, an attractive woman with jet black hair, followed suit.

Damon grinned and stuck to his water. He glanced at the entrance to the bar. A couple stood at the hostess stand where they were led to an empty table. He watched them be seated, waiting for Evie, growing annoyed that she couldn't make it on time like everyone else.

From behind him, James let out a low whistle. "Now she's fucking hot."

Damon turned to look. A brunette, her hair hanging in long, spiral curls, stood at the hostess stand, looking down. A short black dress with one sleeve clung to a rocking body. Her legs were long, her heels high, and if his head weren't still throbbing he could imagine them wrapped around his waist as he pounded into her, hard and deep.

She lifted her head and immediately met his gaze. He found himself looking at a bombshell with pouty bright red lips, cat-like liner around brown her eyes and a knowing smirk on that familiar mouth. "Holy shit."

"I think this is what they call Damon eating his words," Austin said, sounding amused.

"You didn't think she could do it, did you?" Quinn met his gaze, judgment in her expression and she was right.

"No, I did not."

Before he could say more, Evie sashayed across the room, every male eye on her as she headed directly towards him. Her stare locked on his, she stopped in front of him.

"Hi, honey. Sorry I'm late." And with that pronouncement, she sat down *in his lap*, wrapped her arms around his neck and settled her mouth against his.

He stiffened in surprise and she slid her tongue over his bottom lip, causing his cock to rise and his mouth to part. Next thing he knew, he'd gripped her neck, pulled her tight against him, and was kissing the hell out of her in public.

Damon had made out with many females but he'd never wanted to get lost inside a woman the way he did with Evie. Evie. Jesus. Sanity threatened to return but she ran her fingers through his hair and he forgot he'd been about to pull back. He slid his tongue over her lips and speared inside once more.

A whistle broke the moment and Damon jerked his head back, taking the pain as his due. What had he been thinking, devouring Evie in a place he frequented often? It was one thing to test the theory of them being plausible as a couple, another to stake a real claim on her.

"You didn't tell us you had yourself a hot woman," James said. "Keeping her to yourself?"

Damon drew in a calming breath. His dick wasn't cooperating and he was certain Evie felt it against her thigh but he needed to sell *them* and now was the beginning.

"We were keeping our relationship quiet but after Damon's injury, we decided life's short, so why hide our feelings?" Evie spoke before Damon could jump in with an explanation. "Right honey bear?"

He caught himself before he glared her way. He cupped his hand on her thigh. "Right snookums."

From beside him, he heard his siblings stifling laughter. But he had to admit, he'd underestimated Evie Wolfe. She could definitely pass as an NFL player's girlfriend and he didn't mind having her acting as his.

Want even more Carly books?
CARLY'S BOOKLIST by Series – visit:
http://smarturl.it/CarlyBooklist

Sign up for Carly's Newsletter:
http://smarturl.it/carlynews

Carly on Facebook:
facebook.com/CarlyPhillipsFanPage

Carly on Instagram:
instagram.com/carlyphillips

About the Author

NY Times, Wall Street Journal, and USA Today Bestseller, Carly Phillips gives her readers Alphalicious heroes to swoon for and romance to set your heart on fire. She married her college sweetheart and lives in Purchase, NY along with her three crazy dogs: two wheaten terriers and a mutant Havanese, who are featured on her Facebook and Instagram. The author of 50 romance novels, she has raised two incredible daughters who put up with having a mom as a full time writer. Carly's book, The Bachelor, was chosen by Kelly Ripa as a romance club pick and was the first romance on a nationally televised bookclub. Carly loves social media and interacting with her readers. Want to keep up with Carly? Sign up for her newsletter and receive TWO FREE books at www.carlyphillips.com.

Made in the USA
Coppell, TX
02 July 2020